DARK HEARTS

ALIZA MANN

Interior format by The Killion Group
http://thekilliongroupinc.com

ACKNOWLEDGEMENTS

To my Ryan, YaYa and Justin:
I love you more with every beat of my heart.
To the GDRWA girls, thanks for never
giving up on me or allowing me to give up on
myself.

CHAPTER ONE

There was never a bad night to hunt. Particularly when the girls at Harbor U were so plentiful and ready for the picking. Mitchell Rowland, or Mitch, as his friends called him, scoured the living room of the Alpha Beta Omega Fraternity House. In the midst of the air thickened from marijuana smoke, Mitch prowled for all the bad girls. The bad girls – easier to shake loose and willing to forget long nights that led nowhere.

Men from the Rowland family did better the longer they managed to stay single. Despite his predilection for the young ladies at Harbor University, he'd remained just that, thanks to a few clever excuses and a whole lot of elusive maneuvers. As much as he enjoyed the company of a few of them, it was just safer if he left them alone. While some of them didn't like his decision, it just had to be that way . . . unless he found another werewolf or some other supernatural. Supernaturals were as difficult to find as four leaf clovers. From what Mitch could tell, the clovers would be a lot less trouble.

So far during his two-year college experience, there'd only been one person who fit the bill—but

Bridget was like a sister. A strong-willed, witchy sister. Thanks to her and her potions, he'd managed to keep his secret safe.

His whole life had centered 'round needing to keep his secret safe and ensuring that women weren't the reason he ended up dead.

A scene reminiscent of an old school *rave* played out before him as a hundred or so members of the student body gyrated to the pulsing, hypnotic beat. Everywhere he looked, he found bodies in motion—two boys on one girl, two girls acting out a Katy Perry video, dudes in every corner of the room watching as some random chick popped and shook her ass in front of them, and any other combination one could think of.

Mitch loved being out on the weekends. It was a rare opportunity, considering he worked in one of the local restaurants. Jesse's Rib Shack, where Mitch was a short order cook, didn't afford him many weekends off. Bridget, or Gigi as he'd nicknamed her, must have been feeling generous. She was his manager at the restaurant, and she preferred to keep him out of trouble if she could, but every now and again, she took mercy on him.

Best not waste it . . . he thought. Women were a wonderful distraction from a life of secrecy and it's own brand of loneliness.

The woman for the night hadn't immediately jumped out at him yet. Lauren Dillion was there, but he'd hit that so much, it had become annoying. As sweet as she was, he didn't need to keep poking the bear. Sleeping with a woman more than five times who had no shot at being anything more to him was a no-no.

Too many of his friends and family had suffered from falling in love, and Mitch wasn't in a hurry to become the latest victim. Or worse . . . to have the woman of his dreams be tortured or killed for the ultimate crime of loving him. So he kept them at bay, refusing to share his life, or his heart.

Mitch had learned that the hard way. Too late to keep Katie Lynn Delmar from dumping an entire bag of Domino sugar in the gas tank of his beat up Jeep Wrangler, as if it wasn't a sad enough sight. He'd known it was her since he'd just dumped her the night before and she kindly left the empty bag on the ground next to his recently deflated tires and written 'Screw You' with a tube of red lipstick on the windshield in her signature bubbly handwriting. He'd been paying for that break up for months, and still wouldn't be getting his car back from Joe's Auto Repair for another week and a half. Fortunately, Katie Lynn had transferred to another college at the start of the semester, otherwise Mitch might have still been being terrorized.

The outcome was far better than if she'd found out about him. As a result, each day he put on a suit of armor to guard his heart. Falling in love made you take too many chances. His mother and father had found out the hard way. Neither of them were human and it'd still ended tragically. Mitch hated the demon race as a result.

His initial scan of the hazy living room had turned up empty. No one had captured his fancy and there was nowhere else to look for women since the chill of the early fall air was already nearing the freezing mark.

Since the *KLD* experience, as Derrick, one of his roommates, referred to the victimization of his truck, marauding for girls took on a whole different light. Not only did they need to be funny and engaging, Mitch also looked form signs of crazy in their eyes. If the past was any indicator, he should have started that practice long ago.

There was no shortage of psychotic women at HU. He wouldn't have even considered attending if it wasn't the only acceptable school for people like him and the members of his pack—if they were interested in college at all. With vampires funding operations, Harbor was renowned for supernaturals all over the world. Even still, they all needed to keep a low profile. Most of them used some form of magic to camouflage their varied scents. Not Mitch, but those who were concerned with blending more than being true to their species made it a frequent habit. For him, it was more of a matter of safety than *blending*. His mother used to call it passing – as in passing on your history, your culture to assimilate with people who would never really accept their kind anyway.

Mitch studied molecular biology. Finding a control to stave off some of the ales of his kind was paramount, while still maintaining a good camouflage. Harbor provided the necessary cover. And a person had to be pretty fucked up to choose to live in Michigan's Upper Peninsula during the winter months.

Add to that the magic surrounding the Upper Peninsula, and you had one mixed up bag of nuts.

The whole scene reminded him of an old movie his mother used to love with a man who'd dressed as a woman. She used to take him to the midnight, cult-like screenings. Those days were gone though. He was supposed to be a man. Longing for the safety and comfort of his pack would need to be pushed aside. Otherwise, he might as well pack it up, tuck his tail and head the hell home. Control had to be a factor in his day to day life.

It was an epic night had his head been in the game. The Blood Moon was coming. If he didn't want to destroy a whole town, he needed a remedy. Gigi was his only hope.

"Sup, loser?" Derrick had all the appeal of a lion—a loud-ass roar and living purely off his base instincts. He stood immediately in front of Mitch with a beer in his hands and rocking back and forth in his half-dance, half-cool way.

"Sup, dude," Mitch responded. "Where's everyone?" he asked, elevating his tone to rival the loud music on their side of the room.

"Giving zero fucks . . . looking for sorors in a sea of sorors. And the river is full of fish. Lots of bites. Hopefully all of 'em 'll be good," Derrick said. He had a tendency to view women as one-dimensional objects with a hole in the bottom. Even Mitch wasn't that big of an asshole.

With a stifled laugh – more at his fucked up perspective than at his lame joke, Mitch scrubbed his hand over his face and lifted his chin in the direction of the dance floor. "Man, I've fished these waters before. I'm looking for something deeper. You know," he said.

Derrick cocked his head sideways and gave him the grin that he usually saved for professors when he was about to be an ass. "You hit the bong too, huh? All right. I'll see you later. We can talk after your trip to Mecca. Later, homie," he said. Derrick turned and walked away in his designer ensemble that would have taken Mitch a month of working at the restaurant to pay for. Probably cost more than his engine repairs, if he were to add it all up.

"Deuces . . ." Mitch was already scanning again, looking for something more interesting than being mocked by Derrick.

Then he found her. She stood alone in the corner, a beer in her hand and a mischievous smirk on her lips. She was captivating. Enough to make him start moving toward her without really even being aware of it.

Primal and assured, he continued walking in her direction despite the warning in his gut. The fitted white dress seemed to illuminate in the dark. She was a ray of sunshine—her dark mocha skin against the cotton dress arrested him. His dick throbbed and his throat grew dry the closer he got to her.

And fuck yes, her eyes were loaded with all kinds of crazy. They seemed fake almost. Brown nearly celestial eyes. Long legs ran into purple shoes that were encrusted with iridescent stones. She had full lips and high cheekbones. Her curly brown hair looked like it belonged in a commercial or something, each strand swirling its own special way as it seemed to have a brilliant mind of its own.

It only took him about thirty seconds to realize it didn't matter what her eyes looked like. He needed to *be* with her. It was as if her soul extended itself to him. Her heartbeat echoed in his ears and he cursed his heightened senses for feeling the blood in her veins wind through his own.

Why the fuck was she just standing there like she was average, completely oblivious to her goddess status? What would he have to do to possess her? If only for one night, he needed to control her. Mitch would find out if he could just reach her. And touch her soft skin. Breath the same air with her.

Time stood on end, crawling by and belaboring his trek to her – his own heartbeat in his ears. When he was finally standing in front of her, he realized how tiny she was – petite and delicate, yet the strength in her eyes spoke volumes. She was no mere woman, yct she was every bit sexy and lithe.

Mitch raked his eyes over her curves, her heartbeat in tandem with his own. He was utterly captivated with this vision and no words would come out of his mouth. There were so many ways to start the conversation, but none fit the mood. It needed to be something related to capturing her, possessing her soul, keeping her from the world so he could worship her. All of the shit he thought of fell on the stalker-maniac side of the street.

"Are you just going to stare or are you gonna talk to me?" she asked.

Mitch normally thought of girls as angels, but in her case, her scent screamed she was definitely not. Something about her was sinister. Down to her DNA, she was calculating, but her eyes read kindness. A goddamn walking contradiction.

"Hi, I'm Mitch," he said. "Um . . . What's your name?" Mitch knew he sounded stiff and contrived, but in his current state, it was the best he could do. How people stripped definitive lack of confidence from their voices when they were nervous, he would never know.

"Kayla. It's good to meet you Mitch." Her mouth labored over the words. He was lost in her full, sensual lips. She didn't extend her hand and almost looked bored.

"Can we step outside for a moment? It's hard to hear you, and something tells me you have things to say that I might want to hear."

"I can hear you fine." She took a sip of her pinkish colored drink. He wasn't even sure where she could have gotten a wine glass. The party only had red plastic drinking cups, as per usual for campus parties.

Mitch surveyed her, completely unsure of what to do with her next. Most girls didn't hesitate to do what he asked. A challenge. It was nice to run into one for a change

CHAPTER 2

Kayla Tanner had told herself that she wouldn't get into any trouble. Bridget had warned her not to get involved with the boys on campus. And she was to especially avoid the sexy ones since they usually had something extra under the hood. She'd been Bridget's friend since she'd arrived, and with the assistance of Bridget's witchcraft and multiple safety wards at the bridge to keep her father at bay, Kayla had managed to stay out of trouble.

She knew right off. This Mitch was trouble on a stick. He had the swagger of a street guy, the looks of an actor, and the body of a god. When he'd walked up to her, the awkward moment of silence had made her want to jump him with both hands and feet. He sent her demon intuits into overdrive.

Something about him cracked her exterior. "Really, I'd rather stay inside. And you still haven't given me a good reason to still be speaking with you. Sooo – what's up," she asked, glancing around the room. There was no sign of demon handiwork, so she relaxed a little.

Mitch stepped into her personal space. Inhaling deeply, he stared at her. Unlike most men, he focused on her face. "At the risk of sounding like a dick, you're what's up," he growled.

His eyes were different. The deep, cold blue of them reminded her of her father. Alchoe, her incubus father, had those eyes, along with the rest of the male demons. But, this Mitch wasn't a demon, but she could tell that he wasn't fully human. He hadn't even taken care to hide his scent. His dark hair languished in his face, making him look somehow both deadly and safe. "That was classy," she said, battling the urge to smile. There was no reason for her to give him even an inch. Oh, how she wanted to anyway.

This man stood before her, seizing her and making her want to latch onto him. His deep-set eyes were Superman blue with an icy edge, framed by thick, full brows, giving him a sexy, dark look. His jaw line was pronounced. Thick tufts of dark brown hair framed his face, the close-cut sides highlighting his chiseled features.

Her panties were suddenly moist and uncomfortable as he leaned into her, too close. She inhaled, the scent of sandalwood and forest filled her space.

"If I had a choice, I would apologize. Doesn't seem that I do. I noticed you from across the room. You're . . . different than the other girls," he said.

Kayla stepped back, if for nothing more than to catch her breath. His broad shoulders and strong arms would feel so good around her. "Not sure that's a compliment. Is it because I'm black?" she asked. While it was trite, she needed to toss him something to throw him off guard and regain some footing. Her breath caught in her throat.

A scowl lit across his face, further deepened his eyes. They darkened and smoldered, a clear indicator she'd pissed him off. *Just like her dad's would . . .* "I think you know that's not what I mean. I took you for cooler than that," he said, the scowl on his face nearly audible.

Kayla had moved as far as she could away from him into the corner. Leaning against one of the farthest walls, she placed her hand against the other to steady herself.

"I know. I just don't really like being called different," she told him. It was honest and came out before she could stop herself.

"Kayla, you're beautiful and you make me feel something. That's very rare." Instead of responding, she shifted on her feet and leaned further away. He recovered the small bit of space she stole between her and the wall. Taking a deep inhale, he ran his eyes over her face. "But, I need to ask you something," he said. His body heat was palpable against her naked thighs. "Are you a demon?"

It was the first time anyone at the school had made her. Between the witch hunters who'd kill anything that wasn't human, the *seekers* who seemed to pick a different species to kill off weekly, not to mention the Catholics, her life was way too tricky. As luck would have it, she only had minimal powers. "Half. My mother is human," she said. As soon as the words left her, she wanted to kick her own ass. It was too dangerous. In addition, Mitch hadn't done anything to make her trust him.

"Oh . . ." He continued to look at her, brows knit together in a curious frown. Too closely for Kayla's comfort. He could see through it. She knew from the burn deep in her soul.

Kayla looked away from him, the weight of his glare off-putting. Across the room, people were drunk and dancing. Before long, someone would call the police and the party would be ending. It was the way it always happened, and since the police usually came with some asshole *Seeker*, she didn't usually go to the parties. "Are you a threat to me?"

"Not unless you're a threat to my pack. I'm lycan. I shouldn't even be telling you that," he said.

"Well, join the damn club. But um . . . I've never met a wolf before," she said, thankful they could whisper and still hear each other. It was hard to play the game with human guys at loud parties.

"I haven't met a half-demon, half-human before. It's usually all or nothing."

"So, what do we do now? As of a few seconds ago, there was only one person on campus who knew."

"I have an idea. That is, if you're down for it."

"What's that?"

"Come have a few drinks with me. I didn't chase you across the room to confront you about what you are. I really just wanted your phone number," he said with a laugh.

Kayla looked at him, his face softened with a smirk as he finally backed away and leaned against the other wall, a piece of wallpaper shredded near his face. The contrast of his smooth white skin and the dark, torn fabric was remarkable, perhaps not to most, but to her, there was some comfort in seeing tattered shreds shored against his humanity.

He had to easily be one of the tallest men at the party. "All right," she said. When she walked closer to him, it was her turn to take a whiff of him. While she'd known werewolves existed, she'd never met one. Her mother had tried to keep her away from other supernatural beings. A damn lot of good that did. Kayla had been a wild girl in high school. If puberty was bad for humans, it was a triple threat for demons. "You seem different, too." After her statement, she brushed past him and walked in the direction of the kitchen through the entangled bodies on the dance floor.

Kayla could sense him behind her, the heat coming off him registered at a thousand degrees against her skin. Everything was more intense to her. Perhaps it was the ache just beneath her skin that begged for human touch. It was horribly difficult to steer clear of connection to another. But maybe Bridget was right. It wasn't worth the trouble with so many things that could wrong.

She reached the kitchen and placed her empty glass into the sink. To the left, some sorority girl was puking into the garbage can. Grabbing one of the fifths of vodka and two red plastic cups, she turned to find Mitch right behind her. He continued to invade her space and seemed determined to push her over the edge.

"I know where we can go, Mitch. But tell me, are you afraid of heights?"

"Will you be there?"

"Yup," she said. Her mouth went dry and she licked her lips to moisten them.

"Then it doesn't fucking matter," he said.

Kayla loved his foul mouth and the way he spoke his mind. Sin appealed to her, as much as she tried to change the fact.

"Follow me," she said.

Secretly, she wished she could read minds the way some of her kind could. It sure as hell would have made her life easier. She wondered what he was thinking about. If it was just sex or if he wanted a connection. She desperately longed to be a part of someone's life – as opposed to be terrorized by the one connection she *did* have.

The pulsing music had only grown louder since they'd been talking. The bodies had become more and more entwined. There was a haze of lust in the air, mixed with sweat and sin. Someone had lit another blunt and the scent of marijuana added to the cloud of iniquity.

The stairwell held two or three newly united couples as they made their way up the flights of historic steps in the old mansion turned frat house. The fourth floor held the attic ladder. The flights of stairs had ended and all the furniture was covered with huge white tarps. She walked to the middle of the hallway and looked up to see if she could find the catch to pull down the stairs. The music didn't quite reach them and in an instant, it was dark and still. "Can you catch it?"

"How'd you know about this place? I've been here a few times and haven't been past the second floor," he queried.

"It's my power. I can sense things. Usually, it's trouble coming and how I can get out of it. Tonight, I'm not really looking to get out of trouble."

CHAPTER 3

Mitch followed her voluptuous ass all the way up the stairs to points unknown. And he would have followed her to hell is that's where she was headed. She spoke to him. A vice tightened around his heart the more time he spent around her. Even if he never touched her, he knew she would turn his world upside down. It was sex. Or maybe it was more than just sex. The exact thing he feared – that it was more than just sex. He felt his heart lift when she spoke and a gentle tug in the pit of his stomach when she laughed. It was a terrible situation – to be a man on the verge of being overcome when he had everything to lose.

Three shots of liquor in, he really didn't give a damn about anything else. No one had ever made his breath catch in his throat. Even with all he'd seen, and couldn't un-see, she surprised him. Goddamn if he didn't wish it were just her fucking legs shortening his breath.

At the top of the final flight of stairs, she turned to look at him, then up at the thin wire cord hanging from the attic door above them.

Taking the cue, he pulled the cord down and a cloud of dust surrounded them. There was no telling when it had last been opened. Kayla coughed a bit, and Mitch found himself wanting to kick the attic's ass for harming her. "Sorry about that," he mumbled. Stretching to reach the bottom rung of the ladder, he pulled it down and placed it on the floor, pressing on it to ensure it was stable.

"It seems pretty stable. Do you want to go first," she asked. In the dim light, he couldn't see her face, but he knew she looked sexy as hell. Shadows from the dusty windows allowed streams of moonlight to hit her face in shards that stretched across her cheeks though plumes of dust at they swirled about in the air.

"Hang on, you can go first. Ladies always should," he said, and then stepped to the side.

Kayla sauntered over to him and handed him the cups and bottle. The scent of her perfume grabbed him, and without any ability to fight against his animalistic instincts, he grabbed her.

She didn't resist as he seized her, pressing his mouth to her own. Her petite frame against his felt as if she were made for him. Mitch pulled her close to him, deepening their kiss, sinking his free hand into those wild curls. Her hair was as soft as cotton and he delighted in the contrast of her strong will and yielding body.

Her hands slid around his waist and beneath his sweater. Running her fingers midway up his back, she pressed her sharp nails into his flesh. The sting of it only forced him further into her mouth. She tasted of mint and vodka, a sweet and sharp mix, an indulgence he didn't mind.

When his head started swimming, he pulled away, completely unaware he'd stopped breathing. Kayla ran her fingers through her hair and smiled. "Wow, you're good at that," she whispered.

"I could easily say the same for you," he said.

She turned to start up the ladder. Mitch couldn't resist a gentle tap on her ass as she passed him. He followed her, careful not to drop the bottle of liquor on the way up. The ladder had steep steps and he needed to concentrate to ensure his large feet fit into the rungs and he didn't fall backwards. It was no easy task, considering her inviting ass was wiggling just inches in front of his face.

When she reached the top, she disappeared into the darkness of the room. By the time he hauled himself onto the landing, he found her with candles in hand and a box of matches.

"You sure you haven't been up here before?" Mitch asked as he swiped away the dust he'd collected on his pants on the trek up.

"I told you," she said in a singsong voice, "it's just a sense I have."

Mitch smiled at her playfulness and walked hunched over so he wouldn't bump his head on the low ceilings. He found a blanket in the corner and walked to the center of the room to spread it on the floor in the clearing.

After he sat down, Kayla came over with the lit candle and knelt on the floor in front of him. Her white dress had splotches of dust on it, and there were a couple of smudges on her face. She looked damned good dirty. The thoughts that ran through his mind were all of him sullying her more.

When she was settled, he stared at her. She'd taken the cups and was pouring their drinks. She passed him one and then drank hers down in one stiff gulp.

"Kayla, huh? Where'd you get that name?" he asked and downed his own shot. The burn down his throat made him fight back a wince.

"Like a million girls.. I thought about changing it, but now that I'm older, I like that it's kind of unique," she said. Her hands were already moving toward his cup to pour him another drink. "Wanna play a game?" She bit her lip shyly after asking.

"Nah, don't change it. I suits you. Anyway, I don't play games much. Don't know if I can stand it," Mitch responded. He wanted to crawl all over her and was barely controlling his inner beast as it was. Every second was agony. Especially after the kiss that was more intoxicating than any of the liquor he'd drank that evening.

"You can. Call it an exercise in control." She giggled.

"Okay. What do you wanna play?"

"Truth."

"Truth or dare?"

"Nope, just truth. If you don't answer, you have to take a shot. Deal?"

"Deal."

"I go first. What are your parents like?"

"Um, my father's dead . . . When she was pregnant with me, a demon or a seeker killed him. Sometimes, her story changes between the two. My mother lives with the pack and is very overprotective since his death." The pain of that fact threatened to bubble to the surface. Mitch caught it before it could overcome him and pressed it neatly down into his internal backpack of bad shit that had happened to him and his family because of who they were.

"Seekers hunt your kind too?" Her eyes softened in the warm glow of the candle.

"Nuh uh. My turn. Are you close to your father since . . . he's a demon?"

She rolled her eyes, the pain in them so evident it was palpable. Mitch could bit back the urge to hold her, scrubbing his hand through his hair instead.

"I'll drink," she said. Instead of picking up her cup, she drank straight from the bottle.

"Okay. Your turn then," he said. Mitch leaned onto his side, watching her. With her every action, his attraction grew more and more.

"So again, Seekers hunt your kind, too?" she pressed on.

"Yes. The pack moves every now and then, but as we've learned to hunt down their kind, the attacks are growing fewer," he responded. "Are you evil?"

"I think we're all evil to a certain degree. I just have a little harder time controlling mine," she said.

"Let's go a little lighter. What's your major," he asked.

"Theology. Ironic, right?"

"A little. Mind if I ask you why? It doesn't seem like you'd want to study religion."

"Call it curious. It helps me understand all this. It's hard to be a demon estranged from other demons and not be curious, you know?"

"You aren't the least bit concerned that modern religion and its origins may be impacted by the beliefs of the men who wrote it?" Mitch watched as she rubbed her hands through her hair, shaking her head in disagreement.

"Seems like you're getting all the turns," she laughed again. Taking a deep breath, she leaned back on her elbows in a sensuous stretch, her back arching. Pulling her knees in, she sat upright and wrapped her arms around them. Her wild mane fell forward and nearly covered her eyes. "Are you tired of playing this game?" she asked, her eyes somehow flashing him in the darkness beneath lowered lids.

Kayla stood before him, slipping her dress from her body. In a black lace bra with her firm tits spilling from the cups and a pair of matching lace panties and placed her hands on her hips, legs spread wide in what could only be explained as a dominant position. He could see the print of her vulva protruding, the split of her making him hard.

"Yeah, you could say that," he said, his voice barely recognizable to his own ears.

"Take off your clothes," she whispered.

Had he not been able to hear so well, he would've sworn he misheard. As she opened the clasp on the front of her bra, he couldn't move, even though he knew he should have been naked by then. Instead, he watched as she bent to slide her panties from her legs. In the candlelight, he couldn't see her essence spilling from her, but he could smell the faint scent of longing wafting on the air.

When she was completely disrobed, she lay beside him. The angles of her face, the curves of her body – breasts, thighs, everything - worked together to taunt him. Leaning in to kiss her, he sank his fingers into the warm, lush moisture of her slit. Her sex was hot and drenched. Removing his hand, he fished out a condom and slipped the package between his teeth as he hurriedly took off his pants and shirt.

"Want me to help you with that?" she asked. The shy girl look in her eyes betrayed the skillful hand resting on his cock, stroking and massaging as she purred to him.

He felt like a virgin in front of her as he nodded his head, anxious to see how she would assist him. Leaning back, he watched her rip the package open with her teeth and tuck the condom inside the 'o' shape she'd formed with her lips.

By the time her mouth reached his shaft, Mitch was already struggling to control an encroaching orgasm. It was going to be a long, rough night if she could make him come with a single look. And Mitch welcomed it with open arms.

CHAPTER 4

Kayla took Mitch's cock to the very back of her mouth as she rolled the condom down his shaft. The primal waves of lust rolled over her as he groaned in appreciation. His hands smoothed her hair into a ponytail and craned her neck, she assumed to see the diligence of her mouth.

His desire radiated from his body into her psyche and encouraged her to show him her skill level. In the days of Catholic school—back when her mother still hoped to pray the demon from her—she'd learned that the mouth was for much more than eating. She'd corrupted several altar boys in the back of the church after smoking half a pack of cigarettes.

Mitch was so good. His kindness glowed around him, morality radiated from inside out. Her senses cut through the bravado, misogynistic attitude to the core of his heart. If she ever were to collect souls, as her demon father hoped, Mitch would make a piss poor candidate. She'd seen his kind before. His guard firmly in place to block out pain - so thick no human could see through the snark and quips. No, his heart loved people, but he couldn't allow them to get too close for fear they'd weaken him, shattered his oh-so-necessary barriers.

They would have their one night and then it would be time to move on. No good could come from the situation, especially with her many troubles that Mitch didn't deserve.

With one last deep stroke on his penis in the back of her mouth, she rose and pressed him backwards with her hands splayed over his strong shoulders. Mitch sprawled out on his back and allowed her to have her way.

She crawled up his body and straddled him, the hard wood beneath the scratchy blanket made her knees uncomfortable but she wasn't focused on the mild ache. It was pleasure she was after, if only for one night.

The flickering candlelight danced across his face and she raised her hips to allow his cock entry. It had been several months since she'd been with anyone, and the moment the tip of his cock reached her vulva, heavy with need for him, she flinched as she stretched to accommodate his girth.

Stabilizing herself, she leaned in to kiss him once more, missing the taste of him. Kayla didn't move her lower body for a moment, needing to get used to the full feeling of his shaft deep inside her.

He was sweet to the taste, her greedy mouth exploring him. He moaned again, mimicking her. It was one of the most erotic moments of her life, and time stilled around them as she lost herself. His hands spread over her back and ran rough fingertips over her skin, resting them on her waist with a firm, yet gentle grip.

She lifted her body from his chest, but before she could sit straight up on his cock, he grabbed her breasts, one in each hand, and sucked one deeply while he fondled her other aching nipple. Her core tightened around his shaft and she began to slide up and down, rocking on the arch in his penis, allowing it to massage her most erogenous zone.

Mitch moved one of his hands further down her back until he reached her ass. With a gentle pop on the flesh first, he slid his fingertips towards the orifice and stroked. Kayla tingled, her body breaking out into a cool sweat that was hot on her skin.

"I like you, wolf-boy," she whispered in his ear after she leaned in and nibbled on his lobe.

"And I like you back," he said, a guttural groan following the statement.

The sound of sex interfered with their conversation. Kayla rode him, her knees grinding into the hard wooden floorboards of the dank attic. Twisting her hips, she pressed to allow him deeper, and deeper still. Mitch filled her and just when it was too much, too far, she rose and fell again, hard on his engorged, stretched cock.

His tremors shook against her thighs, triggering an eruption deep inside her and a cool sensation washed over her once more.

The quickening of her pace wasn't something she could control. She needed his shaft inside her, the smooth gliding in and out of her body like she needed air to breathe.

The white heat between them was near blinding in its intensity. Her knees trembled along with her thighs as she tried to continue. Mitch's hands flew to her hips and pulled her down onto him, offering some type of unconscious aid to her fevered motion. Again and again, her pelvis collided with his body.

Kayla needed to orgasm before she spontaneously combusted. Her heart beat in her chest as if she were running at top speed. If her brain had been working, she would have realized she was panting and writhing, abandoning the humanity she'd been struggling to hang onto.

"Kayla . . ." Mitch called out her name in a croak. His face contorted, his mouth slightly open struggling with unspoken words.

"Yes, Mitch . . . For tonight, I'm yours . . ." The statements came out scattered, just like her thoughts. They bounced here and there, over the moon and into the dark cool night, arriving at the bright, shining sun. She was vapid and damaged, yet fulfilled and sustained.

Their heated dance ended with her in a heap on top of him and his arms wrapped tightly around her body. Her head pounded suddenly, on the right side, then the left behind her eyes.

Oh no, her subconscious cut into her moment of bliss and euphoria. All of Mitch's sadness, loneliness and distrust of anyone outside of his pack poured into her. It was happening. The threat of a mate bond hung dangerously in the distance. More dangerous was the fact that Kayla had no idea how they worked.

As much as she wanted to stay there forever, she knew she had no business with Mitch. She tried to move away from him, but he held her fast. She was immobile—not only was she spent, but she was trapped. It was the warmest and safest she'd ever felt. "Mitch, I can't. I have to leave," she gasped.

Kayla allowed herself to stay a moment longer, fighting against the urge to flee. She spread across him and listened to his breath as she rode the rise and fall of his chest.

"I don't normally do this, Kayla," he said.

"What? Sleep with random girls?"

"No. Care when they're ready to leave. I don't want you to go. We need another hour, or a few more minutes. You don't want to leave. I can feel it. I know. I know you." He wrapped his arms around her waist, pulling her back into his warm embrace.

"I can't give you another second. I'm no good. You are. As much as you want to be bad, it's not in your DNA. I can feel the good radiating off you. I'm part demon. The two don't mix," she responded. Hot tears streamed from her eyes, across her cheeks, and dripped onto him.

"Just give it a minute. I promise I hear you, and I'll let you go. I just want to stay here for a little while longer. Can you do that? We can pretend you aren't who you are, and I'm not who I am, if it makes it easier."

"It won't matter."

"Try. It will. Just another few minutes."

Kayla knew it was a bad idea. He'd bonded on her, and there was no practical magic that would be able to change that fact. But she gave in, anyway. Wrapping her arms around him, she sank into him. His heartbeat sounded in her ear and she accepted him, his warm body, the tickling hairs on his chest, and the tangled mess they made together in the middle of the floor, on top of a party where a million people swayed. It didn't seem possible that none of them had felt the violent eruption of their union.

CHAPTER 5

Jesse's Rib Shack was only moderately busy in the early evening hours, but Gigi was still on level ten, amped to hell about the two call offs and a late arrival. The heat burned into Mitch's knuckles from the grill as he flipped the quarter pound beef over and lightly poked with the tip of the spatula. There was no excuse for an overdone burger, in his mind. He avoided looking at Gigi. The glare in her eyes was bound to be intense and accusatory.

"I don't know why you want to go down that road again. She's not for you, wolf-boy."

Mitch choked down the disdain at his best friend's comments with a smirk. "Who says?"

"Kayla is not what you need. Leave her alone, Mitch. I mean it," Bridget said with a huff. Picking up her tray, she turned and flipped her midnight black and white-streaked ponytail over her shoulder, then sped off to yet another table of hungry, possibly drunken college students.

On her way across the room, she dropped off the fries he'd just prepared to the curly-haired beauty at a table in the middle of the room.

Mitch may have been prepared to ignore Kayla and heed Gigi's warning, but then it happened. She smiled . . . bit her bottom lip, then ran her hair through that wild as hell, sexier than fuck hair of hers. His mind ran back over the night they'd shared a week prior. She captivated him.

Her smooth, brown skin radiated with a warm blush as she spoke some quick statement to Gigi. It could have been *'thank you'* or *'bring me another trough of fries'* or whatever. Regardless, she looked like an angel.

Mitch returned his attention to the grill, the scent of the burgers reaching the overcooked point that demanded he stop daydreaming about the beautiful girl who'd managed to do what an entire campus full of women had tried and failed at. Miserably.

"Where's my chicken tenders and fries, Mitch? C'mon, keep up with me. We're down a server tonight, so stop poking around." Gigi's voice echoed into the kitchen from the small serving window, which also served as Mitch's vantage point for the whole dining area. Jesse's was an endless source of entertainment.

"Intense, much? Here. Take your order," Mitch barked in his playful way and placed the heated plate from the steel countertop. "And you should try to keep up with me. There are three more behind this one."

"Remember what I said, Mitch. Besides, she already has a man in her life making things difficult. Not only that—you're just too different. So take your break outside before the next rush. And don't even think about bringing those bedroom eyes into the dining room. Leave my orders up."

Another flip of her ponytail, and she was off again. Mitch didn't need to be psychic to pick up that Kayla had been having a bad time, what with all of Gigi's hints and their conversation the night they'd met. And she was right. The last thing he needed was a demon bringing unwanted attention. They could be messy. Mitch was mostly invisible to everyone on campus. Except for the women who went for the tall, dark and arrogant type. The façade he depended on made his life more difficult, but he needed it. His survival depended on it.

He wasn't rich like Garrett or Derrick, the guy whose parents owned their condo. Hell, Michael was even a vet. To everyone, he was just a dude working his way through college with a single mother who scrimped by, sending him whatever money she could.

Gigi was right about another thing. With all the orders waiting in the window and no new ones spitting out of the docked printer synced to the wait stations, it was a good time for a break.

Mitch hung his black apron on one of the tall silver kitchen racks and headed toward the back of the restaurant. Stepping into the evening air, he took a deep breath and stared up into the dark night. "Too much trouble," he whispered in the cold, silent cloak of the Harbor night. A plume of smoke billowed into the air, the scent of cigarettes strong and spicy.

"What's too much trouble? Me?"

The voice seemed to come from nowhere and all around him at the same time. He looked to his right to find Kayla leaning against the dividing fence between the parking lot and the back of the restaurant. Her fitted North Face fleece hoodie and dark gray jeans framed her curvy body, making Mitch's cock twitch.

"Hi. Uh, you know. Tests and stuff." Mitch could have kicked himself for not hearing someone walk up on him. He did have heightened hearing, after all.

"Oh, okay. You didn't tell me you worked here. With Bridget. I didn't even know you knew her."

The moon and yellow floodlights mixed to make everything manila beige. "Yeah, I'm a cook. That wasn't one of your questions."

"Small world. I should have started eating here before. Maybe I wouldn't have so many bruises on my knees from that dusty ass attic."

Mitch regarded her warily, fighting to keep his eyes off the subtle cleavage between the half zipped panels of her jacket. "A joke. Good."

"It's not funny," she laughed, "but I still love cracking jokes." With a shake of her head, she craned her neck to look off into the distance, her brows furrowing and betraying the crooked smile on her lips.

"You're right. You're not funny at all," he quipped. He could have kicked himself again for his dry ass humor.

"Sure, says the guy who has no smile unless he's about to get lucky," she giggled. She dipped her head briefly; the mane of soft locks flowing forward and back again with the sexy neck movement before she turned to him once more. A quick blast of something fruity teased Mitch and radiated around him. He sensed her heating up, which was odd, considering the bitter cold of the winter night. It was even weirder that he sensed anything about her at all.

"Right," Mitch said, the cold, damp leaves on top of his boots forcing him to move his feet to generate a little heat. "Have you always smoked?"

"No. I mean, I would have kept it up when I was seven, but my mother kept finding packs of smokes in my lunch box and taking them. Kind of made things difficult."

"Okay." Mitch was being bested and prayed silently it would stop. He kicked his foot at the mound of snow on the ground. *Shit, she smells good.* Mango? She smelled like mangoes.

"I'm kidding. I think I started last semester. I had a killer course. Introduction to the Old Testament - Hebrew. The stress of it finally pushed me nearly to the brink. Thus, the cigarettes. It's a really bad habit, though." She waved her hand with the cigarette and her scent hit him again. The cool winds carried her magnificent smell on its back and straight to him. The things coming to mind weren't even rational.

A bite. A caress. Warm, sensual hands touching him everywhere. The vision danced across his mind without warning.

With each whiff, Mitch was in heaven, if it even existed. It was often something his kind pondered. "It is."

A shrill, agitated voice came from behind him inside the building. Gigi was calling for him in her *I'm-going-to-kill-you* voice. He was still looking at Kayla, waiting for her to say something. She took a long puff from her smoke and raked her eyes over him.

"I'd better get back."

"I know," she said.

"I'll see you around." Mitch turned on the narrow stoop and opened the back door to head back into the kitchen.

"Yeah, see ya," Kayla called behind him.

Mitch was already facing the other way and trying to decide whether or not he should continue walking with his dick in his hand. He'd never been incinerated before, and an intoxicating girl had done it with one fleeting night, a few lame jokes, and legs that made him imagine the back of her thighs and ass poised in the air as he pounded his cock into her.

"What did I tell you?" Gigi's voice took on a tonal quality that always meant she was pissed.

Mitch stepped into the heat of the kitchen, unsure of whether the source was the grill and fryers or Gigi. "Keep your voice down, lady. Listen, I went out back, just like you asked. She was out there smoking when I got there."

"I get it, Mitch. She's hot or whatever, but you have got to listen to me. This is bad news for you. Between her father and your inability to control yourself, you are asking for it. Need I remind you, *it* is never good? And what would happen if you get arrested? Arrested during a full moon? Do I have to remind you that you still can't control yourself?"

"No, Gigi. You don't. But that didn't stop you, did it? I'm out. I didn't lay on the charm, if that's what you're worried about. I barely spoke. What about her father?"

"What?"

"You said her father as if he was causing her some problems. Is there a problem," he asked, fighting against the caged beast clanging against its cell from deep inside his subconscious.

"It's fine. Nevermind that," she said with a loud sigh. "I should have gone to that party. I should have told you. Does she know about you and your . . . *condition*?" Her hands flailed and rattled two pots hanging on hooks from the ceiling in the middle of the kitchen.

"Yes, but that's about it. Now, if you aren't going to tell me about her father, go back out there, put on your waitress smile, and serve the customers. Jessie will kill us if the orders get backed up. Anyway, Derrick just walked in. I know how much you love waiting on him."

"We're not done. And can't his rich ass find somewhere else to eat?"

"He's not that bad. Go. Wait tables. I'll cook. It'll be great."

"Jerk," she snorted, before storming off to be the best fucking manager-slash-waitress Mitch had ever seen.

Gigi was almost funny when she was angry. She was eleven months older, had only known him for two years, and somehow had become his mother. She was working on a potion to help him control himself. The beast in him was relentless during the full moons. The animal would wake him in the early morning hours, forcing him out of his house to tear into the dark woods.

He really did owe her. Listening to her was something he'd never had a problem with before. Mitch just didn't want her to find out that her opinion was valued and even wanted. He would have never gotten any peace.

CHAPTER 6

Kayla staycd outside for a few more minutes. She could hear Mitch and Bridget arguing. About her. There was no way she intended to be with Mitch again. Even if he invaded her thoughts during class. Even if for seven whole days, she'd thought of him naked at least twice a day. Even if she'd masturbated and came, screaming his name into the night. She had been so glad her roommate was out late that night.

Despite all that, she hadn't tracked him down in the student directory. The fact she'd come out at all while he was on his break was purely based on the foreboding she'd sensed moments before.

The negative energy stirred in the trees. The husk of demon lingered on the wisps of air surrounding the restaurant. She'd felt a mild stirring earlier that day, but when she went out to eat, the eerie sensation ended up in the very spot she hadn't wanted it to.

Near Mitch.

Her father was around. She sniffed the air and brimstone singed her nostrils. He was close. Just over the bridge.

He hadn't liked her heading off into the world, and as much as she wanted to believe he would leave her alone, he'd just as soon kill her than to let her stray away from the darkness. Her mortality had always sickened him.

"Go away. I'm not leaving here," she shouted into the night air.

"Alive or dead, you'll be back." The haunting whisper came from the trees. In the distance, one of the trees on the edge of the forest turned white with frost. The crackling could be heard across the empty field.

Kayla dropped her cigarette onto the ground and snuffed it out with the toe of her hiking boots.

Once more, his voice rose from the dark of night. "He's bonded to you. Tsk, tsk. What will you do now?" he whispered from the trees. In the distance, his raspy laughter shook her to the core.

Turning around, she nearly tripped over her feet getting back to the front of the restaurant and into the golden lights of the dining area. The heavy, wooden door swung closed behind her with a loud thud. The bells hanging on it sounded out, but not before she was back at her table.

"Enjoy your smoke?" Bridget was at her table, dropping off another refill.

"Yeah," she murmured.

"Listen, I don't mean to get in your business, Kayla . . . okay, yeah, I guess I do. You can't do whatever you and Mitch are doing. He's not stable enough and you have enough problems. It's not that I don't believe in love—believe me, I do. I just don't want either of you to get caught up and hurt. What if the Seekers found you both? His father died. They have killed some of your friends. The more of us they collect, the more dangerous it is. Let alone a couple. The bounty goes up," she said in a harsh, low voice.

"I hear you. But you didn't even ask why I went out there . . . my father was here," she said.

Bridget slid into the booth across from Kayla, the red leather of the seat squeaking as she did. "He was? He came across the bridge?"

"No, he didn't. But he was there. He did a *Frozen* number on a tree and coated the goddamn thing with ice. And he spoke to me."

"What did he say?" Bridget asked, her eyes wide with fear.

"He said I'm leaving here, dead or alive," Kayla responded.

"Well, shit. That's scary as hell. At least he wasn't able to get to you," she exhaled and sighed, shifting her tray to one side of her body and twirled her ponytail on her finger. It was her tell for when she was nervous.

"I have something else to tell you. He says I'm bonded."

"What?" Bridget almost yelled the question. "Is it true?"

"I felt it too . . . or something. I mean, I got the headache and I could feel . . . more of him. My mother was in denial about what I was, and I've never been around other kids . . . like me. So, I really don't know for sure. How can I know?"

"Did you dream of him?" Bridget stared at her, the frustration evident in her clenched teeth.

"I did."

"Can you smell him?"

"Um . . ."

"Think. Can you smell him right now? If you think of him, can you see what he's doing?"

"I can do that anyway."

"You sense things. Can you see him?"

"No . . . I can't. But there's an order up. He just put it in the window. It's like I can see what he sees," she said. Kayla closed her eyes and watched as he flipped burgers on the grill.

"I think you guys are in really big trouble."

"Do you think my father knows who Mitch is, or if he just knows I'm bonded?" Kayla asked, a lump forming in her throat.

"He could. We'd better keep our eyes open," Bridget said.

"Should I tell Mitch?" Kayla wondered if it could possibly help if he knew. But something about telling him about a demon who wanted him to die didn't seem kosher. Her head banged a little with tension.

"No. Absolutely not. It can't help the situation. Mitch is a hothead. He'll try to help, and with a werewolf, a demon, and a witch in town dueling it out, someone is bound to notice. Let's just try to figure out how to get rid of your father. He can't get across the bridge, so let's not make things worse."

"I don't know, Bridget. Mitch could be a target," she pleaded. Lying, even with all of her horrible traits, was something Kayla hated doing.

"I know. But, no good is going to come of it. You can't know this yet, but he's stubborn as a mule and twice as ornery. But we'll think of something. Now eat your damn fries, drink your pop, and concentrate on how to rid yourself of your father," Bridget said, as she rose from the table, grabbed her tray, and marched off to help a table full of guys from the basketball team. They were being jerks, but Bridget knew how to handle them.

There was nothing else to do for Mitch. Bridget was right. If something happened to him as a result of her father, Kayla would never forgive herself. That night at the party, she'd known she wasn't supposed to sleep with him. Her senses were on high alert, but something about him made it impossible for her to resist him. He was sexy. He smelled like a warrior and those dark, lush locks hanging all over his head made her weak. In her stomach, her heart, and her head, he was present from the moment he stepped in front of her that night. And there he remained.

After gobbling down her food, Kayla pulled a crumpled ten-dollar bill from her black purse and tossed it onto the table. The best thing about Jesse's was its cheap food.

Kayla looked over at the kitchen. Mitch wasn't looking at her. He was busy preparing orders and tossing completed meals on their plates into the window for pick up. Longing overtook her in an instant. The ripples in his muscular arms made her mouth go dry. She imagined she was one of his utensils and he was using her any way he wanted.

Forcing herself, she stood and walked out the door, concentrating on putting her feet one in front of the other and getting the hell away from Mitch Rowland. He was too much, and too much was more than she could bear.

CHAPTER 7

The sounds of his moans filled his ears. Allowing his hands to roam, he felt her long hair and the heat of her body.

The moans urged him on—his name whispered into the dark room tugged at him in his groin the moment the sound reached his ears.

She wanted him. He was inches away from a treasure trove of magnificence in a tight, hot little box.

Her frame was thin, but she wasn't Kayla. This wasn't Kayla. Fluttering his eyes open, he found a woman crawling all over him. But she smelled different. Her skin was . . . different. Had to be a dream, so why not indulge?

"Kayla . . ." he moaned as his mouth curved into a smile.

"Who?" The angry, screeching voice sealed it. It was definitely not Kayla

With an audible sigh, he grabbed her with both hands and pushed her off him. "What are you doing here, Lauren? In my bed."

"Wha . . . what the fuck, Mitch?" She backed away from Mitch and glared. Her brows tangled into a confused anger, the twist on her lips lit by the streetlight streaming into his bedroom.

"Who let you in? No . . never mind. It doesn't matter. You have to go." Sitting up, Mitch found his shirt and pulled it over his head before even making it all the way off the bed.

"C'mon, baby. You never complained before." Lauren's voice quaked with frustration, as she rolled over onto her back.

Mitch turned the lamp on he clicked on beside his bed and flooded the room with a dim glow.

"It's not you, baby. It's me," he murmured, hoping she'd take the hint and get the hell out.

"That's a line. And it's a load of bullshit that's not even original. My friends told me not to mess around with you because you're so wishy-washy."

"Maybe your friends were right. Listen, I'll take you to dinner when I'm off work again." A lie. But whatever it took to make her leave.

"When would that be, Mitch? Neverteenth of I-don't-give-a-fuck-uary? Don't bother. I'm good."

Pulling on his jogging pants and a hoodie, he stepped into his gym shoes. "Be gone when I get back, please," he said before walking into the hallway.

Mitch allowed the door to click behind him without pulling it into its frame on his way out. Standing in the hallway, he gave his little soldier a light slap. "Sorry about that, bro," he whispered, hoping his penis would forgive him one day.

With another loud, heaving sigh, Mitch headed down the hallway of the condo, finding his way out despite hooded eyes. He was cautious with each step since he was still distracted and confused by what had just happened.

Even a day prior, he would have been perfectly fine with sleeping with two girls within hours of one another, least of all simply thinking of another. There was nothing to attribute to this drastic change. His penis had just not worked for Lauren. It wasn't his first time with her and she was still someone he considered as hot as a closed car on a July afternoon. Perhaps his dick was broken. Like *broken* broken. "Fuck," Mitch yelped, once outside in the crisp air.

Two girls walking past him regarded him with apprehension on the dark night. He gingerly stepped aside, allowing them to pass and attempted a smile, despite his actions erring on the side of psycho. They smiled back, one of them letting out a little giggle. Whether it was his shiny black hair, deep blue eyes, full bright smile, or sleek, muscular build, Mitch knew there were few women who could resist his animal magnetism. He had something for all of them. It wasn't arrogance, just a sense of knowing. Knowing exactly what it took to get a girl out of her underwear.

Laying on the charm for the pretty girls didn't take his mind off his troubles, though. He could play coy if he wanted, but in his heated moments with Lauren, his lust was for another. It was very clear.

Mitch had seen her the day before for four minutes and talked to her for less than two. Her face was the one he'd seen while Lauren straddled him. But he wanted Kayla. Beneath the lights in the restaurant, her skin had shone with a thousand points of light, her radiance blinding him, even as he'd stood observing her with lust and longing from his spot in the kitchen.

The winding paths of the campus leading from one dorm to another blended into a collage of shapes and gray, shadowy darkness. His mind wandered away to their brief conversation and the million things he should have said to her, instead of the ten he'd managed to get out. His body responded to her with every possible reaction, except intelligence.

The brisk air was the only thing keeping Mitch grounded in reality. Having circled the campus, Lauren should have been long gone. Having his car would have made his life easier, but the midnight walks across campus after a conquest helped to clear his mind. Normally. Like when his cock worked and nothing else in the world mattered. Not his propensity to gut another human if he shifted in anger, or having his clandestine life found out by his friends. There was too much that could possibly go wrong for him to muddle over a girl. Even if just thinking of her made him weak.

The lights of the condo were shining bright in the darkened sky, he noticed once he returned. Both Derrick and Michael's bedrooms at the front of the condo were illuminated upstairs. While Michael was probably studying, Derrick was definitely macking on some chick or texting pics of his pecs.

Lauren's car was gone, thankfully.

His key slid into the lock with barely a sound. The last thing he needed was someone finding out he'd fled from a girl into the night like a little punk. Mitch opened the door, swiftly went for the couch instead of upstairs to his room, and grabbed his backpack from the floor in front of the fireplace. The macrophysics textbook was huge and detailed. There was little chance to study for midterms with this woman on his mind and occupying the vast majority of his gray matter. Still, he had to try.

The buzzing of his cell phone was welcomed. Even though his roommates surrounded him, he didn't want to talk to them. They'd just razz him about it, the way he had to them in recent weeks, as most of them seemed preoccupied with one woman or another. Even if he said nothing happened, they'd think he was covering up a poor, embarrassingly short experience.

"Hello, Gigi. I think I'm becoming psychic. I knew it was you before I picked up the phone."

"It's called Caller ID, sweetie. Kayla is infatuated with you. You need to . . . no, you have to fix it," she said.

"From the sound of your voice, I'm sure you're convinced it's my fault. I promise you it—"

"Before you cry me a river, I know all about it. Just stay away from her, Mitch. There's trouble if you don't. I don't think I can get you two out of this type of shit. I'm still an apprentice, remember?"

"Humph," he half laughed, half grumbled. "Well, I'll have you know I was just with a spirited young women a little while ago."

"Stop talking like you're British. As interesting as this all is, I didn't call to tell you about Kayla, or to hear about your exploits. I think I found it."

"The spell?" Mitch sat upright and started to pay attention, pushing his text to the side. There had been so many nasty potions he'd drank in the past few months, Gigi had sworn she wouldn't make him take anymore unless she was sure.

"The potion, and yes. It's a little old, and I've never made it before, but I think it may be the one. I need another ingredient and then we can try it out."

"I hope it's not like the last one. I had hair on my neck for two weeks."

"It's called a beard, Mitch."

"Only if it's on the front of your neck. On the back, it's a sure-fire sex repellant."

"One mistake. *One*. And I'll never live it down. We'll try this weekend. There has to be something to prevent the change."

"So, ah . . . what'd she say about me?" Mitch scrubbed his hand over the back of his neck and sat up straight. As vulnerable as it sounded, the reality surrounding his question was even worse. His palms began to sweat the moment he asked.

"She asked if you were as nice as you seemed. And if you were struggling with some type of neurological disorder." Gigi's laughter brought heat to his face.

"Gigi, that's not funny in the least."

"Sure it is. Seriously, she wanted to know how I knew you, for how long, and whether you have a girlfriend. I told her you were morally bankrupt I think she believed me. Would you stop with that? It doesn't matter, anyway. You can't be with her, Mitch."

"Why do I get the impression you're lying to me? It's just as well. I don't need that shit in my life."

"You don't need it. But something tells me you don't give a damn."

"'Night, Gigi," he said, engaging in diversion.

"Goodnight, Mitch. I'll call you when the potion is ready."

"Cool."

After he ended the call, he placed the phone face down on the couch next to him. It was a cold realization to know his cock may never work again, except for a woman that he couldn't have.

CHAPTER 8

Kayla sat straight up in the bed, the typical burning of eyes that lacked sleep was present and accounted for. She hadn't been able to sleep a wink. Before she laid down for the night, she'd sensed Mitch was with a girl. Then her father had paid her another visit, this time in her dreams. He was a horrible bastard who loved to torment her.

She stepped into her slippers and walked to the small refrigerator in her room. Not even a full week before, she would have been out at a party or hanging out with her fake friends. At barely eleven o'clock at night, she was in pajamas. Something was changing inside her.

At that moment, she couldn't tell exactly what it was for the rumble of anger and jealousy ripping through her. She wanted to call him. To curse him. But what would she say? What reason did she possibly have?

Hey, asshole. Even if we can't be together, I don't want you with anyone else! Somehow, she didn't think he would take that statement well. She'd shut down the connection with a hard mental shield snapping into place before they got vulgar.

Kayla walked to the window. Between her and the windowsill sat a table with a clock and a glass of water, but beyond that was a world of life she needed to live. Was it audacity that made her dream of loving a person who had a good heart? Or was it something else?

Her mother had told her about impressions left behind from others. It was a connection stronger than love, and even life itself. The possibility existed for most supernatural beings—except demons. But what she'd described had made Kayla's heart soar. She had been so young, and as she'd sat there, her wild mane of hair being braided by her mother, she'd wondered if she would ever have an imprint. She wondered if it was even possible. It was so rare that her mother had warned her to just hope for love. To pray for love.

Of course, that was before she learned of her father's blood coursing through her veins. It all made sense. The reason she would break her mother's pathos plant instead of allowing the long strands to run their natural path. Or why she'd cut the bangs off three little girls in her fourth grade class after convincing them it was the only real way they would ever be considered beautiful. And stealing, then wrecking her mother's car in an empty parking lot filled with snow . . . just to see what being out of control felt like.

And at age sixteen, it had all made sense. That was the first time her father came for a visit. And it changed her life forever.

Four years later, in a college full of people who were trying to simply find a new path, she had managed to steer clear of trouble. Until Mitch.

While it wasn't the normal kind of trouble, she was smart enough to know that even if they got together, she would eventually do something that assaulted his very moral fiber.

Her mother had never shared the details about bonding with a mate. Perhaps she hadn't known about it. Whatever. Just one more thing to resent from her childhood.

Taking a sip of her room temperature water, she rolled the possibility over in her mind. It had to be something, considering her father popped up. He always did when things were going well. His proposition was the same as it always was—either come to the Dark or cease to exist at all.

She should have called Bridget. After Mitch was with the other girl, she'd shut down. She felt him. His movement with her. His passion for another. Her powers had never let her feel any other man with someone else. But to tell Bridget the reason she needed to know about imprinting on someone would have been too embarrassing, too revealing. She'd never gotten that close to anyone. *She* was a demon.

In actuality, she wondered if even that was a façade.

Kayla walked away from the window and slid onto the vacant bed across the room. Her roommate was never home. She always had plans and was a cheerleader, and polyamorous, so a single bed wasn't her thing. Kayla didn't mind at all, considering she preferred to be alone when she woke up screaming.

The darkness of the room acted as a cloak. In the dark, Kayla wouldn't confront any of her personal atrocities. The mirror had a way of illuminating her pain. There were no shiny things in the dark. Everything was muted and ordinary. And ordinary was what she wanted most. One day, she hoped, she'd just be a regular girl, dating a regular guy.

Her heart pained as the improbability washed over her.

Her cell phone was on the nightstand and she saw the alarm come on, illuminating part of the room. She stood to go get it and turn it off. Noticing she had a text message, she opened it.

Naturally, it was Bridget.

No matter what, don't contact Mitch. We'll figure it out.

It was like having a mother on campus. Kayla didn't respond. Instead, she opened up YouTube and sorted through her subscriptions. She followed one of the local bands and selected one of their videos. The background looked like Jesse's. The funky combination of jazz, pop, and blues was enchanting.

Don't fall off
Don't leave me alone
Don't forget me when you send me home
I love you too much for that
More than you'll ever know
So don't fall off and leave me all alone

As the words resonated somewhere deep inside her formerly cold heart, she found an image that she recognized in the audience.

There he was. Pressing pause, she watched him. Mitch was standing there in the same clothes he'd had on the night they'd met. His jeans were slung low on his hips and the hard body was evident in his T-shirt. The video was grainy when you zoomed in, but she did it anyway. As pissed as she was about the other girl, she held her iPad in her hands and watched the paused image on screen. He was magnificent.

As much as she hated to admit it, she was going to have to see Mitch. She wanted to break the girl's skinny legs and then beat Mitch to a pulp. She forced the images from her mind and didn't deal with them, but in the dark of night and the solace of her room, she had a different perspective. To find Mitch and let him know he needed to fit her in. No. He needed to choose her.

CHAPTER 9

There was clearly a disconnect between Mitch and his penis. He'd spent all night talking things over with his cock, and had come to the conclusion that his sex life was at an end. After a night of tequila and looking at Kayla's picture in the student directory—and using a sock and some Vaseline to work out his frustrations—Gigi called.

"Get your shit and come over," was all she said. The quick double tone from Mitch's cell indicated she'd hung up.

He rolled over to look at the clock, the dim green glow from the numbers read 7:30 a.m. It was too early. The only other person awake in the condo would probably be Derrick. At least the main bathroom was free. There had been a dance performance on Friday night and Mitch was the only person who hadn't gone. He had been busy searching for Kayla's picture, which had turned out to be worth its weight in gold.

Hauling himself out of bed, Mitch narrowly missed treading on a random pink bra in the semi-darkened hallway. It wasn't the first time someone brought a girl home, nor the first time a piece of underwear was spotted in the hallway. Thank goodness for single bedrooms.

He stared at himself for a moment in the mirror under the über-bright lights in the bathroom. He looked like a wreck. His eyes were rimmed with red and strands of his hair were plastered together and stood in the air.

Mitch scrubbed his hand down his face and leaned over into the sink. The cold water woke him just a little and helped him focus on getting the toothbrush to his mouth.

Stop thinking about her, he chided silently. It would only serve to goad him more. But figuring out what was so special about Kayla was half the fun, if he was honest with himself.

After dressing in faded jeans, a green cable knit T-shirt, brown hiking boots, and a Detroit vs. Everybody emblazoned black hoodie, he headed for the door.

Gigi would yell at him for not wearing a 'real' coat, but it was too early to care.

"Hey, man, 'sup?"

Mitchell lifted his head to find Derrick jogging in place in front of him. He reeked from sweat and whatever he'd done the night before. "'Sup, man."

"Nothing. Just getting my workout in. You should join me sometime. Stop being a lazy bum, you know?"

Mitch looked past Derrick in an effort not to punch him in the jaw. Taking a deep breath, he quickly retaliated, "Yeah, working forty hours a week instead of living off my parents is getting in the way. I've gotta do something about that."

Derrick let out a loud laugh. Sounded more like a bark. "You got jokes, dude. Funny. See you around." Before he was done speaking, he was jogging around Mitch to get into the condo.

Derrick could be a real dick sometimes. Mitch couldn't help but wonder why he worked so hard to make people believe he was callous when everyone knew he had a good heart. It was the guy's saving grace. And Mitch could definitely relate.

Before he could get away, Garrett jogged up. Derrick and Garrett had the same kind of regimen— early and crazy as hell. Garrett was still new to the condo and Mitch didn't wholeheartedly trust him. He seemed to be hiding something, and Mitch would find out one day.

"Hey, Mitch. You got a second?" he asked, mysteriously not sweating from his jog.

"Nope," Mitch grunted. "Heading out, as you can see, bro. I'll hit you up when I get back."

"I just wanted to ask you about Bridget," he said.

Mitch skirted him and resisted the urge to knock him down. "Off limits, bro."

Mitch walked onto the sidewalk and sped up. Garrett had the good sense not to follow him. Gigi was under strict orders not to date anyone in his condo. They were all whores - the lot of them. Nice girls like Gigi would get trampled on.

None of the lights on campus were on as he struck out onto the coiling lanes of campus. The air was bitterly cold, making it hard to take deep breaths. The dead leaves beneath his feet crunched with his every step.

A warm, amber scent reached his nose. As each full moon approached, his senses increased. The next one was in two weeks, which meant he would start hearing and smelling everything. The blood moon.

The scent was familiar and inviting. Mitch glanced around and came to a halt on the sidewalk, waiting to see who would emerge from the darkness. The curvy frame a quarter mile behind him was hard to miss with its jiggling curves and florescent sneakers.

Kayla came up fast, speed walking with headphones on. He couldn't see her face in the low light of dawn, but he could definitely smell her heat.

Mitch turned around and began walking, just fast enough to not look like a creeper, but slow enough for her to catch up to him.

Fancy meeting you here. Lame.

Hey, you look tired. Wanna rest on my lap? Shit, terrible.

I'm surprised to see you walking so fast since you've been running across my mind for days. What the fuck, man?

None of the introductory lines he rolled over in his thoughts would work. He sounded like an old man with a van.

Just be you.

Fuck you, self.

Mitch reached a bench under a tree and decided to take a seat. He had no clue what to say if she asked why he was sitting alone. At the break of dawn. With nothing but a hoodie on. He hoped she wouldn't think he was a rapist. Mitch pulled the hood off to help set a non-menacing vibe.

She was almost in front of him. Mitch focused on the building across the street and tried not to look back in her direction. He could hear his heartbeat in his ears.

"Mitch? Is that you?" she asked. Her voice was ragged from being out of breath.

Mitch turned to face her. She glistened with sweat, which smelled fucking fabulous. Her frame was shrink-wrapped in running clothes, a pink and gray top with the breast cancer logo bold over her left breast, and gray fitted jogging pants. Wild, deluxe curls were piled on top of her head with pink earmuffs stretched across the mass of it. She wore gloves over her hands in the same colors as her outfit. She resembled one of those women's deodorant commercials, encouraging women to sweat like men. Somehow, she pulled it off.

"Yeah. Hi . . ." He had so much to say to her, but couldn't make his mouth cooperate with his mind.

Kayla stood in front of the bench and extended her right leg to the seat next to him. She kneeled over, stretching her hamstrings, then giving him a smile. It was the sexiest damn stretch he'd ever seen.

"Hi. Whatcha doing out here so early?"

"Nothing much. It got a little hot in the house. I needed some air."

"Oh. I'll bet. You live this way? Not in the dorms, huh?" She asked, but it sounded like a statement.

"Nah. Me and some buddies have a condo. Over there, on the edge of campus." Mitch leaned back and pointed at the row of brownstone condos.

"I see. I stay in the Rack. Is it cool living off campus? I would love to, but I can't afford it," she said. Kayla took a seat without Mitch offering one.

"Yeah, it's okay. Is your butt cold?" *Dumb ass. What the fuck???*

"Not yet, thank you . . ." she responded. She laughed a little instead of slapping him.

"I just meant I don't want interrupt your workout."

"Oh. Well, yeah. I guess I'll see you around," she said, standing up and walking in place.

"No, no. I mean, I could walk with you."

"Oh," she giggled. "I thought you were trying to get rid of me. Maybe off to see someone or something."

"No. There's no one else to see."

"You sure about that?"

"Damn sure. C'mon, let's get a walk in."

"Can you keep up?" Kayla asked before quickly stepping away.

"I was going to ask you the same thing," Mitch said and jogged to catch up. From behind, her butt was magical. She was built like she'd been manufactured. Her legs were tight, but her hips and cheeks maintained alluring natural curves. Her waist was cinched, small enough for his fingers to circle if he rode her from behind.

Kayla made Mitch revert into a caveman, his inner beast aching to claim her.

He caught up to her and passed her by, mostly so he didn't have to be tortured anymore with her sexiness.

Each of his steps equaled two of hers since he was several inches taller at 6'3. He slowed his pace, the confines of his jeans around his semi-erection a bit uncomfortable.

"I forgot, I'm wearing jeans. I can't race you today."

"That's okay," she nearly whispered. She was out of breath from their momentary jog. "Another time, I guess."

"We can keep walking. I can make sure you get back to your dorm safely. There's lots of crazy people around."

"Tell me about it. I heard some guy was walking around screaming obscenities a few weeks ago."

"You don't say." Mitch's cheeks burned red. Thankfully, he was flushed from the cold wind, so he hoped she wouldn't notice. They continued on their path and he noticed neither of them was walking very fast. From his perspective, the reason was clear. He didn't want the moment to end.

CHAPTER 10

Now was her chance to tell him she'd been up thinking of him all night. But the words wouldn't come out. Relationships hurt her head. The games and shit were some of the reasons she'd never really tried one on for size. That and her father possibly killing the guy.

Besides, after years of being punished for evil deeds, before long, a person questioned whether they were even worthy of love. And not long after that, they give up on it entirely.

As they walked into the front door of East Rackham dorms, she glanced behind her to see if he was still there. He was. He had the type of swagger that made a girl weak. His body was sculpted. Kayla was even jealous of his clothes because they got to rub against his skin.

"I'm still here, Kayla," he chided. His lips spread into a smile that nearly stopped her heart.

"Just checking," she responded.

"I told you I'd make sure you got home safely, and I will," he said.

"Surely you're aware I can take care of myself. It's the other folks you need to worry about." She giggled at the irony of the moment. She hadn't needed protection from anyone in years, and now she needed it more than ever.

"You never know. It's been crazy around here the last year or so," he said. He caught up to her while she waited for the elevator.

She stole another glance, and sure enough, he was looking at her. "What is it?" she asked, self-consciously smoothing her hair.

"Nothing. You're just prettier in the daylight. I've never seen you this early."

By the time the elevator reached them, she was antsy. The hunger in his eyes was the last thing she wanted to deal with. He'd been bound and determined to accompany her home after their walk. It was completely unnecessary, but adorably chivalrous.

"Well, thank you. You don't have to say that," she said. Stepping into the elevator, she turned quickly to the panel, hiding the mask of disbelief. Would he seriously try to make her believe she was more than a one-night stand?

"I mean it. I have to tell you, I've been thinking about you. A lot. I mean, there's no reason for it, other than I want to be around you," he said, following her into the confined space.

He was standing at her back. Over her shoulder, she could smell the remnants of soap and cologne, a magical combination on him.

"Um . . . I know you're seeing someone," she said. It came out without her permission or consent. Once it had, she turned to see his reaction.

"I'm not seeing anyone," he said. When his eyes shifted to look at his shoes, she knew he was holding something back.

"Who was the girl then, Mitch? I . . . sensed you with someone last night," she said in a rush before she lost her nerve.

Mitch's eyes widened and then relaxed. He shifted on his feet. "Lauren. The girl was Lauren. And I wish you would have sensed one of my roommates letting her in. I was sleeping. She climbed in bed with me. And . . . I honestly thought it was you. I wanted it to be you. But when I woke up and found out it wasn't, I sent her away. I knew you weren't there and while it would have been easy to pretend, I didn't. I want you. I know I shouldn't, but I do. This isn't the best thing for us. I mean, we'll draw attention from someone. It's possibly the worst thing we could do to ourselves, but it doesn't stop me from wanting you."

"I'm *not* in the best place. You're right, it's very risky. But how can I believe you?"

"I don't think you understand. I've always been able to go from one person to the next without as much as a thought. That's not happening for me anymore. Because you showed up."

The slow crawl of the elevator to the fourth floor finally ended and the doors opened. The dim light was replaced with bright sun from the hallway windows.

"Should I come with you, Kayla? Or am I wrong about your feelings for me?"

Kayla stepped into the hallway, holding the doors of the elevator apart to keep them from shutting. After all, if they closed, they may be ending something she'd never even known she'd wanted until he walked into her life.

"C'mon, Mitch," she said, letting the doors go and running her fingers through her hair pushing it back from her face.

As they began to close, he grabbed them, his strong hands slamming them back. She loved the shaggy hair that sprouted everywhere on his head. The look in his eyes that read determination. Kayla backed up to allow him into the hallway.

Turning because she couldn't bear to look at his face any longer without kissing him, she started down the hallway to her room.

It was the fastest they'd walked all morning. She'd sensed him near her dorm and had known when to go out. She'd hoped for just a glance and her heart had danced when she'd seen him. She needed him. The chance at just a glimpse of him had made her jump from her bed to find him.

When they reached the room, she jammed the key into the lock and walked in. He followed and leaned against the door once inside.

She tossed her keys on the bed and sat facing him, hoping he'd follow. When he didn't, she asked, "So, what now? Are we supposed to start fresh? Pretend we're perfect for one another?"

"No. We'll have to figure out how to not get one another killed. Whenever supernaturals come together to form couples, the Seekers find us easier. If they know who our mate is, they can use it against us," he said. His eyes clouded over as he spoke.

"You sound like you have experience," she said.

"My mother and father. When they killed my dad in the street, she had to walk away to save me," he said.

Kayla wanted to reach for him. Hold him. His stoic face and shaky voice didn't match. "She sacrificed the love of her life for you. You have to take heart in that. I guess in a lot of ways, my mother did, too. She loved him as much as you could a demon. But when he wanted to take me back to Hades, she wouldn't stand for it. You see, when you're a demon or chambion, or whatever the hell you wanna call it, you have to choose. At seven years old, I should have been allowed to pick between life on earth or life in Hell, but my mother chose for me. She put me in a Catholic boarding school and left me there. The priests knew. They tried to force the demon out of me. I honestly don't know which would have been worse . . . going through that or being with my father. They kicked me out during my teen years and I had to move back home. And, now, here I am. My father has found me though, and now I don't get to choose. He wants me to come with him. If I don't go willingly . . . he'll kill me."

Kayla spat it all out. All of it. Before she lost her nerve. The only person who knew her whole story was Bridget. She'd sworn her to secrecy and begged her to enchant the Harbor Heart Bridge with some spell or another. She hadn't wanted to. She'd *blessed* the bridge to keep everyone safe, and it really didn't sit well with her to have to place another spell on it. Kayla hadn't had the heart to ask Bridget to do it when the bridge meant so much to her. Perhaps it could have helped, but it wasn't worth risking her first real friendship over. They would just have to deal with whatever came next.

"Would he really kill you, Kayla? I can't imagine a parent being that heartless, even if he is a demon," Mitch came to sit next to her.

His warmth radiated to her body and wrapped around her, the feeling of home and safety shrouding her. "I think so. Are you always warm?" She asked, hoping to reroute the discussion.

"Yes. Lycan body heat is about four degrees warmer than a human. It's our DNA," he responded. "Don't change the subject. I can't help you if I don't know what's happening."

Kayla shifted on the bed, swinging her legs away from him and staring toward the window. "Mitch, you can't get involved. I feel horrible that Bridget's involved. He's not playing around. If you get in his way, he'll kill you."

"The Seekers got their weapons from the demons. In a lot of ways, they're both responsible for my father's death," he said. Placing his hand on her shoulder, he rubbed down her arm.

Kayla closed her eyes, allowing his words to wash over her. "Doesn't that make me responsible, too?"

CHAPTER 11

Mitch could have kicked himself. "No. You weren't even born. I wasn't born. My father was killed while my mother was pregnant. I was stupid for saying that. I wasn't thinking," he pleaded.

"It wasn't stupid. But do you at least see the differences in who we are? It's something we'll have to deal with if we date each other," she said.

Mitch wished she would look at him. He needed her to see him. She had to know he was sorry for hurting her. Kayla was the last person he wanted to hurt. "Kayla, turn around," he commanded.

Slowly, she acquiesced. When he finally saw her, her face was streaked with tears. "Oh, baby, don't cry. I'm so sorry. I keep hurting you and you don't deserve it," he said. Reaching for her, he grabbed her shoulders and pulled her into his chest.

It was then that the dam broke free and she cried so hard her body shook.

"Shhh, it's okay. I'm a dickhead around you. It's because I don't know what to say and this has never happened before. I'll get better. I promise," he said.

Rocking back and forth, he cradled her petite body in his arms and stroked her back as the sobs wracking her body subsided.

"I just don't know if we can really handle this. It's so much, between my father and the Seekers. It's too much," she said.

"It's always been too much. That's what makes it worthwhile. The harder you have to work for something, the more valuable it is." Mitch reached for her chin and tipped her head up. Her face was streaked with tears, her eyes lit up in a sultry, brilliant silver. "Why do your eyes do that?"

"It happens when I'm emotional. I'm sorry. I can usually control myself better, but this makes twice with you," she said, beginning to pull away.

"Damn. I hope you get emotional around me all the time. You're so damned beautiful," he said. Pulling her back to him, he kissed her. Her head tipped back and she sank into him, opening her mouth wide for him to explore her with his tongue.

The taste of peppermint from her mouth made him want to devour her. Mitch closed his eyes, losing himself inside her. She was the most incredible woman he'd ever met. Running his hands down her body, he found the sides of her shirt and lifted it over her head. He broke their kiss to get the shirt off her. "You're like a mood ring. I can't wait to fuck you in a bed." He smiled and tried to make himself look irresistible.

"I can't wait to fuck you anywhere, Mitch," she said in a throaty whisper.

Leaning back from him, she placed her hands behind her back and in seconds, removed her bra.

Her ample breasts spilled from the cups and Mitch focused in on the tight buds perched on their peaks.

Kayla leaned forward and slid her fitted running pants down her legs. She was a vision. Her body was curvy, luring him to her. He reached for her. Mitch's hands landed on her hips and pulled her down onto his lap. He was still fully dressed but couldn't wait to touch her. He ran his hands over her smooth skin, from her shoulders to beneath her breasts, holding them up and nibbling on their tips.

His phone vibrated in his pocket, but he ignored it. It wasn't as if he could stop himself. Kayla moaned softly, whispering his name and the scent of her arousal intoxicated him.

"It's Bridget," she whispered.

"I'll call her back," he mumbled. It was a little unnerving that she knew things without him having to tell her, but now that he had her, he wasn't planning on keeping any secrets from her.

Flipping her onto her back, he pulled at his hoodie, T-shirt, and jeans. His shoes came off in the struggle, and the rest followed. Laying on top of her, he kissed her. The plan was to render her speechless, but it had the same effect on him. He bit at her lips and then kissed away the sting. Sliding down her body, he used his fingers to spread her glistening sex. His tongue lashed at the swollen nub. Using his arm, he managed to press her hips down to stop her wild escape from his mouth. He assaulted her sex, her essence as sweet as her mouth.

Kayla cried out, her legs closing around his neck so tight, he nearly stopped. But he didn't. The goal was simple. He wanted to give her an equal amount of pleasure to offset whatever pain he'd caused. He swore it would be like that for her for as long as she would have him. Even if it was just for one more morning, he would have gladly accepted it as long as she was happy.

The tremble was his first clue she was coming. He pressed forward, running his tongue along the length of her closely shaved slit. Pressing his tongue inside her hot, wet canal, he used rapid movement to simulate his cock.

Her hands in his hair clued him in on her inability to contain herself. To make the moment last, he slowed his pace, another slow lick up the middle and her hands relaxed, the fistfuls of his hair sliding from her fingers.

A few seconds was more than enough. He drove into her again, his tongue stiff and rigid, the friction making her quake. "Mitch," she cried out. There was no 'stop,' no pleading for him to cease his assault on her body.

Kayla raised up from the bed. When Mitch looked up at her, her eyes were nearly radioactive. Kayla's pupils looked as if they'd crystalized from her pleasure.

Mitch flicked her clit twice, three times, then a few more before removing his mouth to finish her with his fingers. It was a devious plot. He wanted to watch her walls came tumbling down.

Kayla shattered on the bed. Her legs flailed and she convulsed. Her mouth stretched open in a moan that couldn't quite come out. She shuddered and shook, her wonderful breasts shaking and nipples so pursed, they looked like pebbles on the beach.

When she was done, she was panting. A gentle hum arose from her, twisted up with sensuality and agony.

"You ready for me, baby? Is your pussy wet for me?" Mitch asked her, his voice foreign to his own ears.

"Yes, please . . ." Kayla cried out, her words finally escaping her.

Mitch obliged, quickly pulling a condom from his crumpled pants on her dorm room floor. He discarded the wrapper, not sure and not caring where it landed, and rolled the latex down his rock hard cock.

It wasn't as good as when she'd done it with her mouth, but it was his turn to please her. Mitch slid his manhood deep inside her. Once he could go no further, he extracted slowly from her tight walls then pushed back in again. Kayla spread her legs so wide he had access to every part of her. Taking one of her legs, he rested it on his shoulder.

They were nearly on their sides in the tiny bed, but he used the footboard to secure himself for the significant pounding he wanted to give her.

For five more strokes, he took it easy. Kayla pecked at his bottom lip, then nipped, then bit, pulling at it, then she sucking it into her mouth, rolling her tongue over it. Mitch fought against the urge to release. It took everything he had to contain himself. But she deserved at least one more orgasm. He needed to hear his name ring from wall to wall and then into the ceiling.

CHAPTER 12

It was more than she could bear. Kayla felt the stretch of her sex, the sensation a heartbeat away from pain, but closer to pleasure. Kayla dug her nails into his flesh, hoping it would provide some sense of control while the rest of her rode the waves of ecstasy. She lost herself in him.

The coolness of her orgasm started at the top of her head and ran the length of her body. She quivered in his arms, her ragged nerve endings near the surface of her skin. She was open and raw.

Mitch wasn't holding back anymore. He pounded into her with jackhammer speed and held her so tightly, she thought she would crumble. The heat of his seed inside the condom warmed her sex. Mitch shuddered, suddenly leaving her body and a cold space where his manhood once was.

His howl emitted into the air and shook her. It was animalistic, primal, and arresting. Kayla did the only thing she could. She pulled him close to her and rocked him. He'd done the same for her moments before. Mitch was on the edge of shifting and in the middle of an orgasm. Her sensory perception fired from every part of her. She comforted him, holding his head close to her bosom and whispering to him. "Stay with me, Mitch. Don't shift."

His body was growing larger with each breath. A blood-curdling wail emitted from a place inside of him she was sure she'd never touch. A change in her dorm room in the middle of the day was exactly what he didn't need.

"Mitch, don't. We're inside a building. You could hurt someone," she said. She shifted to face him, and wondered whether he'd heard her. "It could hurt us, Mitch. Don't change. Stay here with me," she pled.

Kayla reached to pull up the blanket and cover them. All of the bed linens were rumpled at the bottom of the bed, but she maneuvered the mass with her legs until she could pull the blanket over their naked bodies.

He looked so vulnerable.

"Mitch," she said, directly in his face, their eyes locked, "don't change. You can't. Not here. There's a campus full of people." She wasn't lying. There were girls in the hallway and during the early morning hours, people were filing out to work, or to get breakfast, to the library, and everything else.

Kayla breathed a little easier when Mitch's sporadic breathing patterns leveled off. After a few more minutes, the monotone growl subsided.

"I need to get you to Bridget, don't I?"

She waited for his response, not really needing one. She'd already known Mitch was having a hard time controlling his shifts, just from her senses.

"Yeah, I need to go there now," he said in a voice that was still shattered and worn.

"I'll take you. I think you need me to . . . help . . . if the urge comes back," she said, wiping his hair, moist with sweat, from his forehead.

"Thank you," he whispered.

"C'mon. I don't think we should wait." Kayla rose from the bed and climbed over him to get onto the floor. Their skin on skin contact sent remnants of electrical charges through her body and over her skin. She stood up and pulled him up to a seated position. He was so incredibly heavy, he surely was helping her with the haul.

"I know, Kae. I'm coming," he said.

"What'd you call me?"

"Kae. You don't like it?" he asked.

Kayla stood still. Her heart leapt in her chest and she felt weak and stupid at the same time. "I've never had a nickname before."

"Well, I fixed that for you. And, Kae . . . thank you. I've never stopped a shift before," he said. He stood, towering over her. He grabbed her shoulders and pulled her close. The fine hairs of his chest tickled her face.

"I'm here for you, Mitch. I don't want to go anywhere," she whispered as she wrapped her arms around his waist.

"I'm afraid you can't go. Whatever we have to do, we'll do." Kayla began to pull away, but Mitch held tight. "One more second, baby. You feel so good."

"I know, it does feel good. But we need to get to Bridget. She has to find something to help you," she said.

Mitch released her, though she could see the resistance in his eyes. They gathered their tumbled up clothing and dressed themselves. The question that had been burning in the back of her mind since Mitch nearly changed into a full-on wolf wouldn't leave her alone. It was niggling and biting. Completely none of her business, but the past wasn't something she could usually see. With Mitch, there wasn't any exception to the rule.

One the sidewalk, they milled through the droves of kids rushing about. Even on the weekend, there was no shortage of activity. The crisp morning air cut into her skin as they headed down the path. Kayla ran her fingers through her tousled, curly mane. The wind whipped it around her head and she leaned into Mitch, allowing him to be her human shield.

Mitch grabbed her hand, intuitively walking in front of her. His body heat shrouded her, warming her freezing face. They nearly sprinted, just as everyone else did to get wherever they were heading and out of the biting elements.

The deceptive sun was out, but ironically seemed to make things colder. Kayla followed him, realizing wherever he went, the outcome would be the same. The blend of their footsteps clomping over crackling, multi-colored leaves on the ground and the sweet smell of autumn reminded her of what she loved most about Harbor. But Mitch eclipsed it all. He was what she loved most.

Finally reaching Bridget's home, which was a bit off campus, even Mitch's warmth wouldn't help. The twenty-minute walk had been exceptionally uncomfortable, but the primary objective was worth it.

Mitch led her up the stairs of a small, renovated house, stepped up to the door of the apartment and pressed the doorbell. He was still in front of her.

The question. It was back. With a vengeance. "Have you ever shifted during sex before?" Kayla blurted it out before she changed her mind.

"No. You're my first," he said. He didn't look back at her. His eyes remained locked on Bridget's closed front door.

CHAPTER 13

The door of Gigi's apartment was brightly colored and the least witchy thing on campus. Witches weren't really like they were on television or in movies. At least Gigi wasn't.

It finally opened, saving Mitch from the most uncomfortable discussion. He hadn't wanted Kayla to know she'd almost made him shift. Extremes. Those were what he couldn't control. Extreme anger, extreme emotional disturbances, and apparently, extreme longing could all make him change into a hulking wolf. She was a combination of the last two.

"Oh, shit. What did I tell the both of you? Get in here," Gigi said. She was a fireball. Stepping aside, she let the pair into her home. The moment anyone walked inside and up the couple of flights of stairs littered with shoes, the magic crawled all over their skin. Normally, Mitch liked coming by her place, but that morning, she would ruin it.

"Gigi, I'm sorry. I got held up," Mitch started out apologizing as he walked into her flat, releasing Kayla's hands so she could follow him.

Mitch stepped inside her apartment and took a seat on one of the bar stools near the kitchen counter.

"I know exactly what held you up. Look at the both of you. Practically glowing. Kayla, look at your eyes. I told you. I told you not to do this. And now . . ." Gigi stomped around the room, her lithe body making an unbelievable amount of noise on the wooden floor.

Kayla pulled her jacket off and took a seat on the purple couch in the living room. It was all one big room, really. "Bridget, we didn't mean for this to happen. And we can worry about the consequences later. For now, you have to help. Mitch almost shifted a little while ago," she blurted out.

Kayla's face was twisted in concern, her eyes welling with tears. Mitch had no idea why she seemed on the brink of a breakdown.

"What? Where were you? What were you doing?" Gigi's question hung in the air for a few moments. Neither Kayla nor Mitch responded. Gigi stood in the middle of both of them, hands on her hips. "Oh, Blessed Mother. Do you realize what this means?" Gigi paused, running her hands through her hair, which was uncharacteristically out of her normal ponytail. "How did you stop the shift, Mitch?"

Mitch twisted uncomfortably on his stool. Imprinting was something that had seemed so far off. He was still young and wild. "I didn't," he murmured.

"Well, what happened?" Gigi demanded, sounding just like a mother hen.

"I talked him through it," Kayla piped in. "He started the change and I . . . sensed it. I asked him not to shift and he didn't."

"Kayla, this is all very sweet, and it will make a great story to tell the grandchildren, but the seekers will find out about you both, now. Not to mention your father, and, honey, I don't even want to think about those consequences. This is very bad." Gigi took a seat on the couch with a loud sigh, her hands in her hair.

"We're willing to face the consequences, Gigi. If she can talk me out of shifting, then she's bonded on me."

"You think it's you? What if it's her?" Gigi's voice was near a squeal.

"What if it's both of us? I don't know. We'll get through it," Mitch's voice came out closer to a growl.

"I would believe that if we were older and had more control over our powers. But right now, we don't."

"I think the imprinting is the least of our worries right now. It scares me too, but there's no way out of an imprint. We'll have to figure out a way to stay safe. What if we put a stronger spell on the bridge?" Kayla asked. She cringed and shifted to face Gigi on the loveseat.

"I don't want to. That takes me a little closer to black magic than I want to be, and even if we did . . . it's just the bridge. The Seekers have so many resources at their disposal. We can't keep them out. I can't keep them out," she said, exasperated.

"Then we'll fight them if they come. I have to be honest with you, I'm more worried about her father," Mitch replied.

Both Gigi and Kayla sat up to look at him. "Oh, honey, you don't know the half of it. We'd better get busy. Mitch, I made you a potion to try. It'll help you control yourself, but not in anger. I'll have to keep working on that. And Kayla, we'll have to deal with your father later tonight."

"Whoa. Wait a minute. What does she mean, 'deal with your father,' Rory?"

Kayla rolled her eyes at Gigi, clearly indicating Mitch wasn't supposed to know. "I was going to tell you. Bridget and I made this plan before . . . well, before everything happened."

"Everything . . . with me? Even if I didn't know you, Rory, I would help you with something like this. That's just the type of person I am. I can't believe neither of you mentioned this earlier. What's the plan?"

"Mitch, it was my idea to keep it from everyone and that's what we're going to do. We aren't telling you the plan. It's too dangerous. Alchoe isn't a Seeker, he's a demon. A very powerful one. Need I remind you that demons can kill wolves? And witches. And other demons. We can't risk you being there." Gigi stood as she said it.

"Gigi, I don't know where you get off, but let me explain something to you. You're like a sister to me, and if I've really bonded on Kae, you know what that makes her. I'm not staying home and twiddling my thumbs while you two go out and battle a fucking demon. You can chill with that shit. Tell me what happens next." Mitch knew his blood pressure was rising higher from the tightening in his fingers.

"Mitch, naturally I was worried about involving you because I know what kind of person you are. I know you would want to help me with my father," Kayla said. She walked towards him and rested her head on his shoulder.

Gigi stood in front of the couch, not moving. She was thinking, a calculating look in her eyes.

"Okay, so tell me the plan then," Mitch demanded.

"All right, Mitch. One thing at a time," Gigi chimed in. "I need to get your potion. I have one last ingredient to add and then we'll work on Rory's father. Deal?"

"All right, cool," Mitch said.

Kayla took a seat next to Mitch on the bar stools while Gigi went into her closet of secrets and came back out with a glowing purple drink.

"Why is it purple?" Mitch asked.

"That's just food coloring. It adds to the effect," she said with a giggle. "A little witch humor." She set the glass on the counter before reaching into one of the overhead cabinets in her small kitchen. The inlet vibrated beneath Mitch's hands from the potion. Gigi was really good at making potions. She would have gotten an A in it if there were witch courses at Harbor. Well, maybe a B since she'd turned him into half a Big Foot once.

The brown apothecary bottle she extracted looked menacing. When she poured a drop in and began to swirl the mixture inside the glass, there was no smoke or sparks. It just swirled, changing the color to a hazy pink.

Gigi sat the glass down on the counter once again and extended her hand in a welcoming fashion.

"Drink up," she said.

Kayla stiffened beside him and leaned forward.

Mitch pulled the glass toward him and downed the drink, the sweet flavor of grapes and pineapple easing his apprehension. The last potion had tasted like a mix of turpentine and tequila.

"That wasn't bad," he said when he was done. He gently sat the glass back on the counter.

"I'm getting better at flavors, too." Gigi smiled. "Why don't you lay down on the sofa for a second? There's a little bit of a kick."

"Yeah, the last one tasted like gasoline. All right. Come lay down with me, Kae," Mitch said.

"Well, stop drinking gas then, Mitch," Gigi sniped. Another thing she was good at.

Instead of following, Kayla remained at the counter. Her eyes had changed. They were glowing that magnificent silver.

The lower half of Mitch's body felt lead heavy as he stood and stared at Kayla. When his head swam, he couldn't focus on her anymore. While Gigi's apartment was tiny, the distance between the kitchen and the couch suddenly seemed like a mile. Taking another step, Mitch lost his balance and needed to use the coffee table for leverage. He bent down, just two more steps and he'd be on the couch. Gigi . . . had she?

"You drugged me." Mitch managed to get the words out even though he couldn't concentrate on any one thing. He collapsed onto the couch, fighting to hold his eyes open. His last vision was of Kayla.

She was yelling, but he couldn't hear the words. And Gigi was standing there, eyes on Mitch.

Yup, she drugged me.

CHAPTER 14

"Why did you do that, Bridget?" Kayla had been sitting with him on the couch as he fitfully gave in to the magical beverage he'd ingested. She held his hand and stroked his head as he lost his battle with Bridget's powerful potion.

He was a good person. Too good. She hadn't stopped him from drinking the potion even when everything inside her had told her to.

There was nothing about Bridget's actions that were devious. She didn't want Mitch to be hurt. The overarching concern had been to protect him and there was no way to ensure he wouldn't have been killed someone if he accompanied them to the bridge.

"You know the risks, Kayla. We have to focus. This is so dangerous. Come over here and sit down. Mitch will forgive us. I promise. We need to get prepared for tonight," she said.

"How do you know? You gonna drug him into loving me again?" Kayla felt the lump in her throat growing with each word.

"No. I won't. We'll tell him the truth. Getting rid of your father won't be the last of our troubles.

There are hunters and seekers and a bunch of other shit to rally against. This is just the first battle. And Mitch'll live to fight another day. Right now, time is wasting. Unless you've changing your mind on me. You'll need to call your father here, and deal with him. Or, are you ready to walk into Hades and give him up forever?"

Kayla leaned down to him on the deep purple couch and lightly kissed him on the forehead. "Yeah, I'm coming." Kayla straightened and headed back to the bar stool she'd been sitting on. "I don't really have to call him. He's always present. Silently stalking me. I'm the one that got away," she said, referencing her other siblings who would undoubtedly slit her throat just as soon as give her a hug.

"That's kind of a good thing. I found one of my grandmother's passages in the Book of Mourning. It's a spell that weakens supernatural beings when you love them. Whether you know it or not, you do love you father, and that makes him even stronger. His powers will have a greater effect on you if there's love in the mix."

"I do love him. But not enough to give up my life."

"It's okay. I mean, parents are the reason we're here, so I understand the conflict you're feeling. More than you know. Once he materializes on the bridge, he'll be expecting you to go willingly. I need to chant this over and over. You'll have to fight until he begins to weaken. As the spell crests, you'll stab him," she said.

"In his heart?"

"Kayla, demons don't really have hearts. They don't need a soul to survive like humans. You can stab him anywhere, but for good measure, I wouldn't aim for his toe or some random appendage. Get him in his head, chest, or stomach."

"Got it," Kayla agreed. "Can I do it with anything? A stick or a butcher's knife?" she asked. It was only half a joke. As hard as she tried, she couldn't muster a smile. As evil as he was, no one really wanted to kill their father. At least, no sane person and despite Kayla's demon half, her humanity nagged at her to do the right things. Killing could not be considered right in any way.

Fear ripped through her. Finality hovered in the air. Kayla tried to discern whether it would be her or her father's final battle. There was no clarity in her perception.

"No. If it were that easy, there wouldn't be any demons. The seekers use Ruby's Knife."

"Who's Ruby?"

"Not who. It's a thing. The blade must be hollow with a serrated edge. It has to be made of silver and the handle wrapped in some kind of material that will absorb electrical charges to protect the human who uses it. I made one for us. Then I enchanted it for extra protection," she said. Bridget walked back into her pantry, the rustling sounds alerting Kayla that she was looking for something hidden in a secret place. "Got it. You have to make these, so I bought the blade from the army surplus store and the handle is made of animal bone and filled with Spanish moss." Bridget stood in front of her with an object wrapped in white muslin cloth.

Kayla held her hand out to move the cloth away. Pulling her hand back, she looked at Bridget first.

"It's okay. You're half human. It won't hurt you," she responded as if she were the one with deepened sensory perception.

"Okay," she said. Taking a deep breath, she removed the flap and saw the most beautiful knife. It sparkled in the sunlight that poured into Bridget's apartment.

"If you hold it, it'll take on your personality. That's the reason they're so dangerous. It can be used for both good and evil. In your case, since you have the power to be both, you'll have to make a conscious choice to be good in order to kill your father. If not, you'll hesitate. And hesitation has only one outcome for you. You understand, Kayla?"

"Yeah. I do. I guess we'll find out tonight, won't we?"

"That we will. We need to get Mitch back to his condo," Bridget acknowledged. "This place is too close to the bridge. If he wakes up, he could easily find us. With his nose, he'd sniff us out in a matter of minutes. And demons leave a powerful aroma."

"I guess you're right."

"I know I'm right. He should be out long enough for us to get this done. When he wakes up, he'll come looking for us. When he gets there, it'll all be over and we'll explain everything. It'll work like a charm."

"Says the witch who owns the charm." Kayla didn't even try to camouflage the sarcasm in her voice.

"Listen, it's going to be fine. Mitch is reasonable and he'll know that this was super dangerous. We can't have everyone around us while this happens. Tonight is perfect because the Keys' concert is going on and everyone will be there. Stop worrying. You'll need to focus all your energy. Help me pack my bag. We only have a few hours to get Mitch home and make it to the bridge."

"How are we going to get him in and past his roommates?" Kayla hadn't thought of that before. The thought made her nervous. She'd seen the group he hung out with. They were overly protective.

"He'll walk in. The spell on Mitch is extremely vulnerable to suggestion. We can tell him to walk into his house and go straight to his bedroom, and he will. All we have to do is rouse him a little before we say it, and he'll do as we command."

"Glad he's with us and not someone who means him harm, I guess."

"Nothing will happen to him. We're keeping him here until it's time to leave."

"Bridget, I don't know what I would do if anything happened to him."

Bridget looked up from wrapping the knife back up and sliding it into a plastic shopping bag. "I know." She stepped from behind the counter and wrapped her arms around Kayla's shoulders. "I know you'd fight to protect him from anyone. Even me. And you can't even help it anymore. I had to do this. Since you've bonded on one another, there's nothing but magic to keep you apart if one of you is scared or in trouble. This is for both your sakes."

"I know, Bridget. Let's just get this shit over with."

Kayla pulled away from Bridget and turned back to look at the man who'd captured her heart in such a short time. Mitch was the reason she wanted to defeat her father more than anything. For the first time in her life, there was someone other than herself at stake. For the first time, she loved someone she had no reason to. And she would fight to defend her new love with her very last breath.

CHAPTER 15

Mitch woke up in a dark room with something important on his mind he couldn't remember. Someone was knocking on his bedroom door.

"Come in. What's up?" Mitch responded.

"Hey, cuz. You good in here? Why is it so dark? You're not rubbing one out, are you?" Derrick asked with a snort at his own dick joke.

"Get the fuck outta here with that, dude. What's up? I'm not in the mood for your shit today." Mitch was sitting up on the bed, but didn't reach to turn on the light. His head pounded violently.

"Shit, bro, I'm just joking. Wanna talk about it?"

"Not at all," Mitch responded, unsure of what he would have talked about. Kayla emblazoned a streak across his mind. *Where the fuck was she?*

"The only thing that could be fucking with you after sleeping all day is a woman. Who is it? That nerdy waitress? I could tell you had the hots for her."

"Gigi's my friend, man."

Derrick took a seat on Mitch's bed and leaned forward, resting his elbows on his knees. He tried to look thoughtful. It ended up a little smug. As usual.

"So, it's somebody else, huh? Well, you know my philosophy. You need to hit the heavy bag. A few hours in the gym and you'll forget all about this chick."

"Did you forget what you needed from me?" Mitch didn't want to travel any further down the trip to crazyville. Derrick was a lunk. A very, very rich man, but a lunk nonetheless.

"Oh, nah. I wanted to know if you guys could make yourselves scarce this evening. I'm bringing a girl over to . . ."

"Man, yeah. Whatever. Just close the door behind you."

"All right. Shit, I know when I'm not wanted. You want me to leave a pair of your panties on the doorknob so everyone knows you're PMSing?"

"Get the fuck out, asshole."

"Deuces, you little pussy."

While Derrick didn't mean any harm, Mitch was strongly contemplating kicking his ass.

Mitch leaned back onto the bed and rolled over. With nothing else to look at, he stared at the champagne walls in the dark room.

The words '*you little pussy*' echoed in his head. There was something he was unsure about. Who had he seen earlier and what had happened to the day? He was supposed to be heading over to Gigi's. He'd seen Kayla. No, he and Kayla had made love and he . . . had he shifted? His muscles were distended and achy, like he'd shifted earlier in the day.

What was he forgetting? Where was Kayla?

Mitch picked up his phone from the nightstand beside his bed and unlocked it to see if he'd missed any calls. There were none since that morning, just the one from Gigi from earlier. Shit, he was supposed to go take the potion. She would kick his ass for sure.

There was a notification on his home screen. Someone had left him a *Glide* video message. The screen name was *silver22*.

He entered the app and scrolled to the message. Kayla's avatar looked just like her, with a round face and a mane of curly hair that resembled a halo around her head. It was smiling at him.

Mitch couldn't help but smile as he pressed the forward arrow to play the video.

Mitch, I just wanted to let you know that I'm sorry for everything that happened. It's not what I wanted, but it's for the greater good. I'll see you when you wake up and hope that you can forgive me.

Fucking excruciating. Mitch sat up sharply, allowing his phone to fall onto the bed with a thud. What the fuck was she talking about? Another knock on the door prevented him from returning to her video.

"Yeah?"

"It's Michael. Everything okay?"

"Uh huh. Come in."

Michael opened to door and stepped one foot inside. "Derrick said you were going through some *40 Year Old Virgin* shit in here. Doesn't seem like you. I just wanted to check on you."

Mitch couldn't help but laugh at Derrick's joke. The asshole. "Yeah, I'm gonna be all right. Can you talk for a second?"

"Sure, man, what's up?"

"This girl, man. She's everything. Her body is banging. She is on some glamorous type shit, and she seems smart. Like bonus. But . . ."

"There's always a 'but' with somebody that amazing. Shoot." Michael came into the room in all his rocker glory. He was the coolest guy in the whole house. An amputation hadn't stopped him from living out his dreams. It was one of the things Mitch admired about him most. He sat on the gaming chair in the middle of the floor and still looked cool.

"Her father is apparently a real dick. He could cause her some problems. I don't know if I wanna deal with that kind of shit."

"Well, I can understand that. But if it's some other-world-type shit you see in her, you may not have a choice."

"Shit, I'm already dealing with my own messes, man."

"It's just . . ." Michael was the master of staying out of people's lives and Mitch picked up on the fact that he was choosing his words carefully. "You don't usually keep girls around for long. You know what I mean? What makes her different?"

"If I knew that, I would put a cap on that shit. She just stole the air from my lungs the first time I looked at her."

Michael stared blankly at Mitch for a moment.

"You know what I mean, man?"

Michael scratched his thick blond hair and clasped his hands together. "I do. Unfortunately, I do know what you mean. And I'm telling you, if you had that experience, you should go after her. Fuck her father."

Mitch picked up the water bottle from his nightstand and took a long drink. Michael had a point. He didn't quite know how to respond.

"Ay, man, I've got to get out of here. Going to watch my brother's set. But I did you a favor and took those panties off your doorknob."

"Fuckin' Derrick. Thanks, man, and I appreciate the talk, too."

"Anytime."

As Michael stepped out of the room, Mitch stared at his phone. His friend was right. He would have to go after her. He would fight the devil himself for her. And he would have to deal with the consequences, wherever the road to damnation . . . or commitment . . . led him.

Mitch didn't bother with a video message. Instead, he headed for the shower. Whatever she thought she'd done to him, or whatever the problem, they would fix it in person and not using technology. He wanted to feel her beside him and not stare at her through the phone. He needed to feel her against him.

CHAPTER 16

By the time Bridget and Kayla made it to the bridge, the sun was setting. It had taken some time to get Mitch into his condo and back again to get all the supplies. Just one knife wasn't good enough. In case she needed more, Bridget had enchanted a few pocketknives and researched more spells to ensure nothing went wrong.

Daylight Saving Time had made it darker sooner, and just like Bridget had prophesied, the bridge was deserted when they arrived. Bridget parked the Jeep she'd borrowed from a friend near the base of the bridge. It took another hour to draw a pentagram in the hill at the side of the bridge.

Kayla watched as her friend went from a light, airy soul to a master of the dark arts. She had worn a long black coat with tall, black boots that laced all the way up the front of the leg. When Kayla had joked in the car on the way over about her appearance, Bridget had responded, "What's a witch without a bad ass ensemble, right?" Then she sobered. "Fuck, I hate this magic. There's the hint of black spells in it. Just enough to make it unbearable." She cringed a bit.

"I'm sorry to make you do this," Kayla whispered, shame overcoming her.

"It's necessary. Your father and his buddies are responsible for this kind of magic. One less of them to worry about, if we do this right. Now, concentrate," she said.

Kayla refocused on digging the circle around the outer points of the star figure. Cold winds interfered with her efforts, but it wasn't enough to deter her.

"Okay. So how long does it usually take?" Kayla asked.

Bridget looked around assessing the area, "I'm a first timer, so we'll have to just figure it all out." The tone of her voice wasn't exactly reassuring.

She and Kayla stood near the mouth of *Pont d'Amour*. The wind picked up and a whistling sense of death surrounded them. "I think he's coming soon," Kayla said, if for nothing more than to reassure herself that everything they'd been working on since the start of the semester was coming to a culmination on the bridge that evening.

"I think you're right. Are you ready? I have to head to the pentagram. It's the only thing that'll keep him off me. Otherwise, I'm a sitting duck out here. You ready for this?" Bridget's eyes, as strong as she pretended to be, were filled with concern.

"Yeah, I've got this. You go down there and start the chant. We'll need a good head start."

"The knives are in your knapsack. Don't lose sight of it. I don't know how many chances you'll have, but make sure you use the right one the first time. You understand, Kayla?" Kayla opened her arms and threw them around Bridget. The two hugged with the full knowledge that if anything went wrong, it could be the last time they would ever see one another.

When they released each another, Bridget really was crying. "Okay, go get 'em," she said.

Kayla watched her climb down the side of the hill to the safety of the pentagram. Bridget had the huge book in the center waiting for her and opened it to the appropriate section. The low throttle chant began, and by the second time around, the change in the atmosphere was palpable.

It was time for Kayla to walk ahead and meet her potential fate. She would have been lying if she'd said she wasn't wishing Mitch was by her side. But to risk his life was too much for her. As much as she regretted Bridget drugging him and rendering him unconscious, she would also want to die if he were somehow harmed. It was up to her. With Bridget's help, she would have to defeat her father.

Kayla reached the center of the bridge and looked up at the trees around her. That's where his voice usually came from in the physical world. In her dreams he was everywhere, but on earth he was smaller. There were so many forces against demons, their reach was nowhere near what it had been in the past.

She waited. The sounds of the water beneath her and the rustle of wind through the leaves littering the ground around her feet were all she heard except for the chant. Bridget hadn't broke once. The cadence washed over Kayla as she practiced patience and awaited the most deadly being she'd ever encountered.

Pretty girls fall in love, yes? The thin ones with straight, blond hair and golden-bronzed skin from the summer sun . . . the demon taunted. Alchoe was there. The name her mother whispered to her in warning. She was afraid he would hear her call, so her mother had written it down, as well.

The boys flock to them. But not you, Kayla. Surely, you knew before running after that boy. He won't understand, will he?

Just as in the past, the sound of his tattered and drawn voice came down from the trees of the riverbank.

He won't understand your half-demon self, will he? He's one of the good ones. He's not even fully human himself. Not only are you tragically unattractive, but the part of yourself that you try so desperately to hide will be the very thing that drives him away. A shame. I would have loved killing him.

"Leave him out of this, *dad*. This is between me and you," she shouted at the ridgeline on the other side of the bridge. *Mitch*, she whispered in her mind.

The demon continued. *You hear me, don't you, weakling? You should be in fear for your life right now. It's only a matter of time. And never mind your little boyfriend. He won't save you. Remember, you aren't the type of girl that men save. You're the kind they fuck and leave. Alone.*

"You bastard," she screamed. Kayla's voice cracked, exploding from the pit of her sickened stomach. "I want to see you. We need to talk. Child to father. Come here now, you sick fuck!"

I'm the bastard? Lest ye forget so soon. Your mother is the one who conceived you with one of us, which one, she can't be sure. Either way, you should have never been. You're an abomination.

But that's neither here nor there. I'll put you out of your misery soon. It's for the best, really. I mean, you're nothing at all. Do you know that? Nothing. At. All.

As he spoke, the thin outline of a figure materialized and moved closer and closer to Kayla, until his stale breath misted in her face. *Do you know where he is? He's coming to look for you. And when he gets here, he'll find nothing but your remains. Is that what you want for him? Why not save yourself the trouble and come willingly?*

Alchoe was there, but he wasn't. In order to stake him or whatever the fuck you called stabbing a demon to death, he would need to be if full form. He was still too strong. Still not in front of her like he needed to be.

"I'm not coming with you. You can't make me go," Kayla was screaming at him, her voice so loud it rang in her own ears.

Can't I? I could have made you leave this place long ago. It's just a sweeter victory when you choose on your own. That's what I've been waiting for. For so many years, you've tormented the humans. At times, it was fun to watch. Those times when you visited me, fitful and tormented, I'd seen it all.

"I never visited you. You haunted me. I was tortured my whole life and you were the cause."

Is that what you think? No, child. That's not the case. You sought me out. You *control your own mind. It's called free will. You exercised it.* He laughed, his grizzly face taking on color. His flesh was grayish and molten. His eyes were a flaming sapphire.

"I never did that. You. It was always you!" She was screaming again.

The chanting behind her grew louder. The air chilled to somewhere south of zero and her breath showed in a cloud as she screamed into the night air.

You are denying who you are, girl. You are my child. You called out to me. You always do. You are half demon and that part of you has ruled your life from the day you were born.

Kayla steeled herself. As her absent father developed before her like an old Polaroid picture, she watched.

Somewhere deep in her soul, that quiet part of her knew he was right.

CHAPTER 17

Something was wrong. Mitch couldn't shake the sensation crawling all over him. Still hazy, he stood in the opulent, golden glow of the bathroom across the hall from his bedroom. The maid came once a week. Unlike most college dorms or quads, they had shit like scented soaps and framed mirrors in their bathroom. Sconces and shit he wouldn't have known about otherwise. He stepped out of his funky workout clothes and into the shower stall.

After he turned on the faucet, streams of water hit him from all sides, even from below. It was one of his favorite features of the condo.

Scooping water into his hands, he pushed it through his thick, dark hair. In an instant, he saw her face. Most of the time when he imagined her, it was in a beautiful haze, reminiscent of the night he'd met her behind Jesse's.

He gripped the shower wall to steady himself. This image was of her struggling with something. In the thick darkness, she was yelling, her voice hoarse from crying and desperation.

The jagged image cut into his mind without warning and his gut ached from his inability to help her. Just as suddenly as it had come, the vision was gone, leaving in its wake a thick, gut wrenching sense of urgency. Mitch turned off the shower and attempted to process what had happened.

What had happened was a first. His mother had once told him he the power of sight that only came to special pack members, but he'd never believed her.

Mitch grabbed a towel from the neatly rolled sets on the towel bars and wrapped it around his soaked frame. Padding back to his bedroom, he was unconcerned with the mess he was leaving behind him. He needed to get to her. As preposterous as it seemed, Kayla could be in danger.

He stepped into his bedroom and pulled on jeans, a sweatshirt, socks and shoes at the speed of light.

Mitch grabbed his black pea coat from the bed and left the room like it was on fire. He made it down the stairs and saw the dim light of the sitting room, where a fire was going. They'd never used the fireplace.

His promise to Derrick came back in a flood. *Shit!*

He proceeded to walk toward the door, shooting a glance over his shoulder. There was no time to comment on the girl who didn't seem like Derrick's type on the couch. If her clothes were disheveled and she was ripping Derrick's clothes off, the scene would have been more common. Instead, they had books spread over the coffee table and Derrick was discussing what seemed to be a salient point from one of his business classes.

"See ya', man." Mitch didn't wait for him to respond, nor goad him for studying. It was obvious he'd put a lot into his evening, and there would be plenty of time to razz him for his sudden change in choice of woman.

The door closed with a click behind Mitch and leaves softly fell onto the ground. The air was frigid, even more than normal. He wanted to shift into a beast, but he didn't. He fought every one of his internal instincts to save his girl. Barging in as a wolf, or worse, in his naked human form, wouldn't do. He'd scare the shit out of her and there was no concrete proof she was in mortal danger. He wished his vision would have been clearer.

Instead, he charged across the campus, his boots crunching on the freshly fallen leaves, and sharp, crisp air biting into his face as he ran at top speed.

The dorm was lit, the activity of students in the common area spilling over into the dark walkway in front.

Mitch averted them and headed to the side of the brick structure. He gauged the rooms on the third floor for Kayla's suite. The bricks were slick with ivy, but he grabbed on and scaled the building, calling on his superhuman strength to hang on, one at a time. He didn't want to call attention to himself, so he leaned into the building, slowly and steadily climbing.

The thought of a locked window crossed his mind, but it was better than reaching her room and having to break down the door. Word of something like that would spread across campus at the speed of light.

Her ledge, like most of the other windows, jutted out and made for an easy grip. He hauled himself upward and scanned the room first. It was dark, only the glow of her television power button lit the room beneath a blank screen. He searched for Kayla in the darkness, from the chairs to the floor to the bed.

She wasn't there.

Instead of climbing down the wall, he jumped. The four stories of the building passed by him at lightning speed. Mitch landed in a crouching position on the grass.

Walking out to the sidewalk, he glanced up and down the street. The scent of something rank wafted faintly to his nose.

Mitch grabbed his phone from his jacket pocket and pulled it out. Watching the message again, he paid close attention to Kayla's every word.

. . . wanted to let you know I'm sorry for everything . . . it's not what I wanted . . . it's for the greater good. I'll see you when you wake up . . . forgive me. She was crying in the video, her eyes red and puffy.

Her message was strange, but even stranger was the fact that he couldn't remember anything concrete about the day. He'd started out heading to Gigi's.

Another thought shot out from the recesses of his mind. Bridget. She'd been watching him as he fell into a slumber. It wasn't in the dorm, though.

Mitch began walking toward Bridget's house. He struggled to recall the events of the day again. He'd gotten out of bed and headed to Gigi's. Kayla. He'd been with her. And then the image of Bridget. Anger filled him, but he had no idea way.

Finally, the fucked-up, cryptic message Kayla had video texted him made more sense.

Mitch picked up his pace. Getting to Kayla was the singular mission that propelled him forward. There was nothing he wouldn't do to keep her safe. But where was she?

The image from the shower was of her alone. She was outside. It was so dark, nothing seemed to be around her. She was yelling at someone. *But who?*

Mitch arrived on Gigi's porch in record speed for his human form. Only moments had passed.

Raising his hand to knock on the door, another image hit.

He was waiting on her porch. Bridget opened the door and it was morning. She'd had her mad face on. Who was behind him?

Shit, what the fuck? Mitch knew he was too young to have lost a whole day. Something had fucked with his memories.

After a few moments, there was no answer. He walked around the house and sniffed the air. That smell. It was dank, like an old urinal in a baseball park or . . . no, it was the smell of death.

A shudder rattled him to his bones.

In a flash, Kayla was before him again. No, not Kayla. Kae. That was what he called her. She was screaming for her life. And then she was on the ground. Something struck her.

"Kae!" Mitch shouted into the night. He could see her, and then the bottom of a steel girder.

The bridge. Kayla was on the bridge.

The image was gone, and regardless of whether or not he was on campus and someone would see him, Mitch pulled every stitch of clothing from his body. Even though he was pissed off and scared and worried, the shift didn't come. "Fuck," he screamed at no one.

His roar echoed into the trees.

The potion. All of a sudden, he could remember. Bridget had given him a potion. And it had knocked him out. And they were going to fight her father.

Now they were on the bridge, alone. With a demon.

Kayla couldn't die like his father. Mitch would rip her father to pieces with his bare human hands if he had to.

CHAPTER 18

Kayla fought to pull herself from the ground. The slap from her father had been so hard and devastating, it made her knees buckle. He was in full form now. His legs were deformed. He had the body of a satyr. His hind legs were slender like a goat's and his tawny, gray skin was covered with wrinkles. There were horns on the top of his head, but not like from the pictures of demons. His horns were like a ram's.

"You can't kill me, *father*. I won't let you," she said.

The beastly figure stood above her, his nostrils flared and his teeth bared in his scowling mouth, "Oh, but I can, dear girl. If you were to think about it, you'd find that this is something you want. Isn't that the reason you haven't tried to stab me with your bag of tricks? You see, I know everything. And when I'm done with you, I'll send you back to kill each of your friends, one at a time," he said.

Kayla watched her father—the thing that was turning into flesh and bone before her. It wasn't time yet, though. She needed a few more moments.

Reaching behind her, she unzipped the side of the bag and searched for the handle of Ruby's knife. When she had a firm grip, she rose to her feet. Alchoe was taller than her by a foot, his hands long and gangly on his arms.

Taking a deep breath, she slowly backed away. One step, then another. As she moved backward, Alchoe advanced.

"You've ruined my life, but for the first time, I know what it feels like to be almost normal. I won't let you take that from me." She snatched the knife from the bag and raised it into the air.

"Are you waiting for something dramatic? As if I'd shrink away and cower in fear of your little knife? I'm sorry, child. That's not how things work in the real world. That knife doesn't mean anything to me. Come with me, before you have to suffer the mortal pain of dying. There's nothing in me that prevents me from snapping your neck. Right here. I told you before, dead or alive, Kayla. This is your very last chance."

The air grew too thick for Kayla to breathe normally. Choked with her own fear, she panted and attempted to calm herself.

"And I'll give *you* one more chance. If you don't leave me and my friends the fuck alone, I'll kill you. I don't mean that shit metaphorically. I will kill you and walk away as you dissolve into nothingness."

"My, my. Now that sounds more like something a child of mine would say." Alchoe was a second away from her. So close she could scent the brimstone. "I'm almost proud of you."

Kayla steeled herself, another moment and he would be in full form. Just a second more, if she could keep him talking. "You should be. After all, I'm daddy's little girl," she said. Bringing the knife down, the hilt of the blade plunged into his rib cage, just inches away from what would have been a human's heart.

"Tsk, tsk. Too soon. You always underestimate." He slowly pulled the blade from his chest and tossed it to the side. "I'm not fully formed yet, didn't you're little witch friend tell you? She said, *'In your case, since you have the power to be both, you'll have to make a conscious choice to be good in order to kill your father.'"* It was horrifying hearing Bridget's voice coming from his body. With a wicked laugh, he continued, "And clearly, you haven't made the choice."

Alchoe raised his hands to Kayla's neck and wrapped them both around her throat. She struggled to fight against him, but it was futile. He was too strong for her. As he strangled the breath from her body, he lifted her into the air and held her with her head right in front of his. He stared at her, eye-to-eye, and waited for death to claim her. Kayla kicked and thrashed. She grew weaker with each movement.

The last of her will was draining from her body. Giving up wasn't an option, but the power in her to fight was fleeting.

"Give up, girl. There's nothing more to be done," he told her. Even his breath was cold against her skin.

It was a hard fight, but she refused to let him win. There was Mitch. They'd only just started to grow close. And for the first time in her life, she had friends. It had been weeks since she'd done anything bad. And goddammit, she was only twenty. There was so much to live for.

A warmth came over her. It was so safe and familiar. In the far distance, it was coming and she wanted to run to it. *Kae . . . where are you?*

She heard it, but is seemed like a dream. Then again, *Kae?*

Mitch was there. She couldn't see him and she didn't know exactly where he was, be he was coming for her. She wanted to call out to him, but all she had were her sparse thoughts. *Mitch, I love you.* With the last breath of air she had, she kicked her father. In her raised position, her foot sank into the flesh of what would have been a cock.

The bag she'd had was so far away, and with each passing moment, she felt herself floating further and further away from consciousness. She was dying. The stranglehold Alchoe had around her neck was causing her lungs to collapse into themselves.

Bridget's chant was louder now. It was nearly all Kayla could hear.

She closed her eyes to concentrate on it, the comfort of Bridget's human voice lulling her into a deep slumber.

CHAPTER 19

Mitch found them.

He couldn't see Gigi, but he heard her. The bridge was a few hundred feet away. Her chanting was constant.

He looked around, trying to determine which way to go first. He hadn't been able to shift. The cold of the night was cutting into his naked skin. From the trees, he laid eyes on the most disturbing sight he'd ever seen: something was strangling Kayla.

"Kae," he yelled out, a guttural growl.

Mitch took off at top speed, undeterred by the pain of his shift. At first it was reluctant, but finally his beast tore free from his human skin.

In a second, he was fully beast, his long black coat blowing in the wind.

Mitch stopped an inch away from the monster who held his woman. His animal mind was unable to rationalize how to get her free before ripping the thing who held her to shreds. It was a demon, no less her father, but none of that mattered.

Mitch rose on his hind legs and bit down into the demon's neck. He slashed at the monster with his large paws, his claws gnashing at his skin. With a yelp, the demon dropped Kayla to the ground. She lay there, seemingly unconscious, but Mitch needed to focus. Circling, he stood in front of her on his four legs.

His panting was mixed with a growl as he pushed forward. Mitch stalked towards his prey, backing him away from Kayla's limp body.

Demons were dangerous, both magical and strong, but for some reason, he wasn't using his powers. Mitch sized him up and the demon tilted his head, looking at him warily.

"Oh, I see. You're the boy. I must admit, you'd make quite a pet in Hades. We have a few just like you down there. One of them must have been your father. You see, you can always tell by the pelt. When I killed him, he hardly put up any fight at all. And your sweet mother walked away. I was tired that day, so I didn't give chase. But I should have. Had I killed her that day, I wouldn't need to do the same for you now. No matter. I'm versatile. I can adjust to any situation."

Mitch wished he could speak in his wolf form. He would have told this asshole exactly what he was thinking.

Mitch proceeded forward, nipping at his feet. He needed him far enough away from Kayla so he couldn't grab her again during battle. It was an exercise in patience, and Mitch barely had any left. He bit at the demon, wanting to take him apart in small chucks and digest the pieces.

"Listen, dog . . . I'll give you a chance to run for your life. You can either flee now and die another day, or I can kill you here on the bridge. I'm feeling generous today, so I'll let you choose."

Mitch saw red, all cunning leaving him. Raising up on his hind legs, he charged, using his paws to knock the demon over once more. Something had weakened him, or had made Mitch stronger; either way, he ripped at his throat and pulled out a section of it, leaving only half in place.

The demon's hands grabbed at his throat and pain seared through Mitch. Somehow, the demon had cut him and Mitch could see the blood on his fingers as he bit the freak's wrists. With a slap, he pushed Mitch off him and jumped to his feet. Skin from the hole in his neck hung down his chest.

With one charge, Mitch had him on his back again. He used his paws to split open his chest and continued to pummel him. Holding him down by his neck, he continued an assault on various parts of his body, ripping skin from bone. Mitch felt the pull of his fur from the demon's nails, but it wasn't enough to stop him. He clawed into him and silently swore he wouldn't let him get to Kayla again.

The demon was silent as Mitch lashed at him, tearing him to pieces.

From behind him, Mitch smelled Gigi. With one leap, she was over the two of them and came down into the demon's open chest with a blade.

A shrill yell came from the demon and echoed across the sky.

Mitch jumped back. There was a blinding light emitting from the tangled mess. Gigi was on the other side, knocked to the ground from the force. Before their eyes, the demon swelled into a mushy, gray, bulbous lump. Bright red light radiated through the holes in his skin and filled the surrounding area and into the night air.

In another second, the lump exploded. Parts of him scattered, and Mitch backed away from the deafening sound.

Mitch ran to Kayla, still in wolf form, and licked at her face. She wasn't waking up and the fear of losing her consumed him.

Gigi came over to her and began to administer CPR. Mitch backed away, watching, praying his sweet Rory would respond.

CHAPTER 20

Kayla blinked her eyes, her body shivering from the cold. Bridget knelt over her, pressing into her chest. The cough hurt so deeply in her lungs, but she gulped down air in spite of the pain.

"I'm up . . ." she managed.

Bridget stopped her rapid compressions and looked at her. Tears streamed down her face and her electric blue eyeliner ran the length of her cheeks. "Oh, my god, you're back," Bridget exclaimed.

She fell onto Kayla, hugging and kissing her cheeks.

Kayla tried to rise, but everything hurt. She felt like she'd been boxing. The pain wracked her from her feet to her head. "Is he gone?" she managed to ask Bridget, even though she still hadn't caught her breath.

"Yes. With old stubborn ass Mitch snapping at you in all his wolf glory, there wasn't much choice," she said.

Kayla looked to her right to find the most beautiful creature she'd ever seen. His body was covered in deep, coal-colored fur and bright blue eyes stared at her with such pain and compassion, she felt as if she was dying again inside them. "Oh, Mitch . . . you're so beautiful," she gasped. She held her hand out to him. There was no fear in her, even though he was the size of a compact car. He padded over to her, his tongue lolling, and licked her hand.

His warmth was still radiating and overpowering. Kayla sank her hands into his fur and stroked, indulging in the softness.

"Guys, we'd better get off the bridge. I don't know the odds of a Seeker tracking down a witch and two supers on the same night versus us all being nearly killed by a demon, but I'm not interested in finding out. Let's get to the car."

Kayla attempted to stand, but her knees buckled. Mitch was waiting there, catching her with his body and standing still while she crawled onto his back. Bridget gave her a hand with climbing the rest of the way on.

Being on Mitch's back was a lot like horseback riding. Kayla hung on for dear life to the long hairs of his neck as he followed Bridget to the Jeep parked a half-mile from the bridge.

For the first time in her life, Kayla felt free. Despite the pain. Regardless of being unable to use one of her arms without searing heat ricocheting through her body.

Bridget helped her into the passenger seat, then opened the door to let Mitch into the backseat of the truck.

She had to let the seats down so that he wasn't so cramped, but he still couldn't stand in the car. He whined pitifully. "Sorry about this, buddy, but you know you can't walk back to wherever the hell your clothes are," Bridget explained.

Kayla wanted to laugh, but she ached too badly.

Waking up in a strange place had always been disconcerting to Kayla. The room was bright with the morning sun.

Kayla rolled over and found a body next to her. He was warm and familiar. Mitch raised his head and smiled. His brilliant white teeth and powerful blue eyes made her go weak, not that it was a stretch, considering her body felt like she'd been used as an Olympic punching bag.

"Good morning, Kae," he said. He was leaning on his arm and gazing down at her as if she was the only woman to have ever lived.

"Morning, Mitch," she responded. Her voice was hoarse and scratchy, but it didn't matter. She'd awakened next to her most prized possession.

"Morning. You and Gigi have a lot to make up for, but I'll give you preliminary forgiveness since we all could have died yesterday," he said.

She wished she could have laughed, but her chest was on fire. "Can I please have some water?" she asked, giving him a smile.

"Sure." He stood up as she watched. He wasn't wearing anything at all, his stripped down butt muscular and toned. Kayla wanted to grab it, but trying to sit up was a notion she couldn't fathom.

Mitch returned from his compact refrigerator with two bottles of water. Handing one to her, he kept the other in his hand and climbed back into bed.

"Where are you hurting?" he asked, gently.

"Everywhere. My face and chest are the worst," she responded, then took a sip of the water, which tasted a lot like heaven.

"Okay, let's start with the nasty bruise on your eye," he said. "It's safe to say classes are out this morning."

"I don't even think I can move. It's okay. I haven't missed any this semester," she responded, wincing slightly as the cold bottle touched her face.

Mitch held it in place as she slowly got used to the freezing temperature. "Look at you, being the good girl. You can stay with me today. I don't have any tests, so I can miss a couple of days."

A thought passed through Kayla's mind and made her mini-panic. "Will your roommates mind?"

"Please. There's at least one other girl here now," he said. Regret appeared on his face the moment he said the words. "I mean, not that we have a lot of girls roaming through here . . ."

"Mitch, it's okay. I just don't expect anyone else to roam into your bed from now on," she said with a sweet but deadly smile.

"That's not something you have to worry about. You've managed to take care of that for the rest of my life. Do you even know what it means to imprint on someone? I'm sorry, but I'm yours to keep."

Kayla fought against the pain and rolled onto her side and looked him directly in the eyes. "I know what being bonded means. I just hope you realize, I have a dark heart."

Mitch removed the bottle from her face and moved it off to the side. Stroking her hair back, he leaned into her and whispered, "And now, I have one, too."

OTHER BOOKS BY ALIZA MANN

Contemporary Romance -
Disarmed
Stellar Heart

Urban Fantasy -
Fury Rising

AUTHOR BIO

Aliza Mann was always a surprising person. At age nine, her mother grew very concerned when she spent an entire summer only leaving her room to eat and go get more books. She begged her to go out and play, like the other kids, to no avail. At 11, she discovered her mother's romance novel subscription shipment and Aliza knew she'd found her people.

But could she write a novel herself? Throughout her teen and young adult years, she resolved that it was too grand a dream to ever come true.

It wasn't until she was comfortable in her health insurance career, the mother of two beautiful, yet nearly grown children and in a devoted relationship with the man of her dreams that she resolved maybe she could have it all. And so, she did.

Aliza has written several books since making the choice to become an author, in addition to volunteering as President of her local RWA chapter. Each book can only be compared to the birth of a child. No matter the number, there's nothing on earth like bringing life into the world.